# Rose, On Her Own

Michele Pendleton

Copyright © 2013 Michele Pendleton
www.michelependleton.com

All rights reserved.

ISBN 1482569167
ISBN-13 978-1482569162

DEDICATION

For Joel, Jessica, Josiah, Jordan and Justin

## CONTENTS

Chapter One .................................................................................... 1

Chapter Two ................................................................................... 9

Chapter Three ................................................................................ 19

Chapter Four .................................................................................. 22

Chapter Five ................................................................................... 29

Chapter Six ..................................................................................... 39

Chapter Seven ................................................................................ 51

Chapter Eight ................................................................................. 61

Chapter Nine .................................................................................. 71

Chapter Ten .................................................................................... 83

Chapter Eleven ............................................................................... 93

Chapter Twelve .............................................................................. 103

Chapter Thirteen ............................................................................ 113

Chapter Fourteen ........................................................................... 123

Chapter Fifteen .............................................................................. 131

Chapter Sixteen .............................................................................. 139

Chapter Seventeen ......................................................................... 148

Chapter Eighteen ........................................................................... 156

Chapter Nineteen ........................................................................... 165

Chapter Twenty ............................................................................. 173

# CHAPTER ONE

It was early on a Thursday that felt like a Monday, but Rose Millican could only focus on Friday. She daydreamed of a lazy, carefree weekend resting quietly alone at home. June was a hectic month in the wedding industry, and she was tired from her recent career demands. Not to mention bored with the staff meeting currently taking place. She swiveled her chair back and forth in an effort to stay awake since the two cups of coffee hadn't helped. As far as Rose was concerned, attending staff meetings was the only drawback of her job at *The Bride's Side* magazine. She much preferred to spend time behind the lens of a camera rather than behind a conference room table. She had stumbled into her career by accident, as she seemed to do most things in her awkward existence, but her keen observation and natural talent made her an excellent photographer. Antsy for the meeting's end, Rose continued to pass the time by twirling a strand of hair around her right index finger. But soon the boring staff meeting would be the least of her concerns. Life was about to change for Rose, forever.

"As most of you know, we have a fast-paced promotional job coming up that will cover six weddings over a six-week period, and I'll be announcing who receives that assignment next week," said Jeannie Cooper, the magazine's chief editor. Jeannie enjoyed Rose, not just for the talent she brought to the magazine, but also for her friendship. Though she was old enough to be Rose's mother, they got along as well as any two girlfriends of the same age. Other than Jeannie, and her childhood friend Lily, Rose usually forged more friendships with men, which probably explained why she worked so well with her staff partner, Frank Harrington.

"But as for current assignments, there's a photo shoot coming up in San Diego next month, and I believe Rose and Frank should take it," Jeannie said, glancing in Rose's general direction. Several seconds passed before Rose realized someone had spoken her name. She began to move her eyes back and forth as though she were a Wimbledon spectator, and wondered what she had missed while her mind wandered.

"Rose, San Diego next month? Are you on board with me here?"

"Yes, Jeannie. Absolutely. San Diego next month. I'm there," Rose said, as she brought herself back to reality long enough to answer. "Can't wait. Right, Frank?"

"Right, Rose. Can't wait," Frank said as he looked at her and smiled. He secretly adored her, or at least he thought it was a secret. Everyone knew, except for Rose. In addition to being smitten with her since she joined the magazine three years ago, he considered Rose not only his photography partner, but also his closest friend. Frank, ten years her senior and a consummate professional in his field, would do anything for this woman. He followed his response to Rose with a wink, and she smiled back, clueless of his interest in her.

Rose had forgotten to silence her cell phone that morning, and her smile with Frank was cut short when she heard it ring. She didn't recognize the number, but she did notice it was from her hometown. Happy for the diversion, she excused herself from the staff meeting.

"It's my boyfriend, the millionaire again. He simply *won't* leave me alone," Rose joked as she looked at her ringing phone.

Rose made her way to the door past her colleagues who snickered at the remark. Working so closely with a group of people had its advantages and disadvantages. Everyone knew Rose didn't have a boyfriend, much less one who was a millionaire. In fact she hadn't even been on a date in quite some time. But she didn't mind poking fun about her own love life. She hadn't had one in, well, she couldn't even remember when.

As soon as she closed the conference room door behind her, she answered the call.

"Hello, this is Rose."

A timid but somewhat familiar voice began to speak. "Rose? This is Allison."

Allison...Allison...the only Allison who Rose knew was from high school, Allison Saylors. Well, Allison Saylors McIntosh now. Another of the *married with a family* group she didn't fit into yet. As she walked down the hall towards her office, she realized it had been at least two or three years since she had spoken to Allison.

"Allison, it's been so long!" She stepped inside her office and closed the door.

"Rose..." Allison tried to interrupt her, but Rose kept talking excitedly.

"Our ten year reunion is in a few months, Allison, right? I've already put it on my calendar."

"Rose, I need to talk to you for a moment. Seriously, I hated to bother you at work, but this couldn't wait."

"Allison what's wrong?" Rose felt it. That feeling you get when someone is preparing to deliver difficult news to you. "Allison, are you okay? The kids? Your husband? What is it?"

"Rose, we're all fine.

"Then what's wrong, Allison?"

"It's Lily."

Rose felt numb all over. She had a tendency to always think the worst. She reached behind her, feeling for her desk like a blind woman, searching for something to brace herself against. Lily Harwell had been Rose's best friend since first grade. All through elementary, middle, and high school, Lily and Rose were inseparable. No matter what happened in Rose's life, there was always Lily.

"Rose, are you still there? Can you hear me?"

"What about Lily? I just had lunch with her when I was in town last month. I loaned her some money because I knew things were rough for her. I know it was difficult when she lost her job after moving out from Adrian. Especially since he left her with all those bills."

"Rose, I need you to listen to me. I can hardly get this out as it is."

3

Somehow Rose knew, but she waited. And in the silence, Allison finally spoke.

"Rose, Lily is gone."

"Did she leave town again?" Her words made almost no sound, like a sudden onset of laryngitis. She was certain she knew what *gone* meant, and it didn't just mean from town.

"Rose, honey, I'd give anything not to be the one to tell you this, but someone had to. They found her this morning. Her car had gone off the old bridge at the lake. The police retrieved it from the water around sunrise, and she was still inside. A neighbor had noticed the absence of her car and lack of activity for a day or two, so they put out a search. She's gone, sweetie. I'm so, so sorry."

Rose suddenly felt cold, and helpless. "But why would she even be driving on that old bridge?" Rose knew the old bridge was seldom traveled since the new one had been constructed. "Why would Lily have gone there?"

"It looks as though there was no obvious reason for the accident. No skid marks on the road, no signs of foul play either. It's as though she just drove herself off…"

"Don't say it, Allison. Damn it! You know she would never do that! Just because life hadn't been kind to her lately doesn't mean she would…she would…well, you know." Rose could barely speak. She actually struggled to even breathe at that point.

"Rose, I'm so sorry. No one wanted to tell you, but we knew you would want come back home for the funer--"

"Don't you dare say funeral. Don't you dare, Allison. Please, please don't say it." Rose frantically looked outside her office window for someone, *anyone* to help her. But everyone was still in the conference room.

When Rose took longer than expected to return to the meeting, Jeannie became concerned and walked to her office. When she opened the door, she found Rose with her eyes squinted, tears rolling down her cheeks, and the phone held against her forehead. Rose jumped up, handed Jeannie the phone, and ran out of her office. The staff meeting came to a halt as the other photographers ran into the hall at the sound of Rose crying. Jeannie took the phone and closed the door to Rose's office.

"Hello?"

Allison introduced herself and recounted the story she had failed to finish telling Rose. Ever the editor, Jeannie took the seat behind Rose's desk and made notes. She shook her head back and forth in disbelief as she continued to listen. When Jeannie concluded her conversation with Alison, she hung up the phone, and prepared herself to face Rose.

Meanwhile the staff made every effort to calm Rose, who now sat with Frank in his office. She ranted uncontrollably and spoke in broken sentences which made little sense. Inconsolable, Rose finally buried her face into Frank's chest.

Jeannie walked to where they were all gathered around Rose, and asked if she could have a moment alone with her. Her colleagues, some of the very best people she knew, hugged her and stroked her hair one by one as they walked away. Except for Frank, whose shirt Rose held onto like a security blanket.

Jeannie inhaled and exhaled deeply before she spoke. She was thankful for Frank's presence and the support he was providing to Rose. Such news is never easy to hear, but Jeannie needed to convey the additional information Allison had given her. They thought it best if Rose were back in her own office, so they stood up and clung to her tightly as they walked back down the hall. Once in Rose's office, they all sat down. Frank pulled Rose close to him again as they listened to Jeannie.

"Rose, I spoke with Allison. She told me about your friend Lily."

Frank continued to hold Rose. He would hold her as long as she wanted him to, in any capacity. Rose had mostly stopped the crying and shaking, but was still in shock. Frank didn't dare let her go.

"I'm sorry, Jeannie. I shouldn't have thrown the phone at you like that. It was rude of me. I'm sorry," Rose said in a whisper, her throat sore from crying.

"Rose, think nothing of it. And besides, that's not important right now. I need to talk to you about Lily."

"She's dead, isn't she?" Rose asked, though she already knew the answer. She hoped she was wrong, but she knew better. Frank continued to hold her next to his chest, and she clung to him even tighter.

"Yes, Rose, she is," Jeannie said sadly. "You were close to her, weren't you?"

"She was my best friend all through school. We were always together. We grew up in a little resort town by the lake where people vacationed, fished and water skied. We had such wonderful times there. We weren't *as* close after graduation. We wanted different things from life. But I still loved her, Jeannie."

"I know. That's what Allison said. She also said you were very good to her and had helped her out lately. Financially, I'm guessing."

"Well, yes. She hit a rough patch, you know? I thought all she needed was a few dollars and a few hugs and all would be well again. Where did I go wrong?"

"Rose, you didn't do anything wrong. This is one of those truly sad things that happens in life and it's not fair to anyone. I'm sure if she was a friend of yours, she must have been an interesting person. Would you like to tell me about her?"

"Lily…what can I say about Lily? We were *so* different, but we were the best of friends. She was funny and daring, and I was reserved and shy. At the lake one evening when a group from high school decided to skinny dip, she stepped right out of her bikini and jumped in the water, completely uninhibited. I stayed on the bank in my one-piece swimsuit, covered in a towel with my arms wrapped around myself." Rose blushed when she recalled the story, even though it had been years since it happened.

"And Lily was beautiful and tan, while I was plain and pale. She had the beauty, and I had the brains. She had the guys, and I had my camera. She wanted to be a wife and mother, and I wanted to go to college. Recently, she moved into an apartment with a man named Adrian in hopes of making that wife and mother dream finally come true. She thought he was *the one* but he left her after only six months, with debt he had accrued on her credit cards. I don't want to think she did anything to herself on purpose, but…"

"What's important, Rose, is that you be near your friends right now. It's time for you go to back home."

"But Lily was my only *real* friend from high school. I knew lots of people, but Lily was the only one I truly cared for. Now, she's gone. I don't know if I want to even go to the funeral. I don't know if I can face it. And I don't think there's anyone else there I care to see."

"Well," Frank said, "I'm sure many others cared about her as well. You all share a common loss. I think you need to surround yourself with those people right now. Surely there will be at least *one* person you'll be glad you reconnected with once you get there. Rose, you should go."

"He's right, Rose. And don't worry about things around here for a few days. We'll rearrange the schedule."

"Absolutely. It will be fine, Rose. I'll start putting things into motion myself, and I can get one of the newer staff to help me. It won't be like having you here, but I'll get by somehow until you get back," he said, winking and smiling at her.

"I'm so sorry to let you down like that though, Frank. And as much as I hate to admit it, I know you're both right. I need to do this. No, I have to do this. I have to go back home."

Jeannie knew Frank and Rose worked fabulously together. No other two people on the magazine produced their impeccable level of work. She sensed that Frank wanted to speak with Rose alone. So she embraced Rose and then mentioned something about attempting to get the staff meeting back on track.

As Jeannie stepped out of Rose's office and walked back to the conference room, Frank closed her office door. He drew the blinds shut so they had complete privacy. They stood facing one another, and he took her dainty hands and held them together inside his.

"Rose, you know I'd move heaven and earth for you. I'd take all this back if I could. But since I can't, I'll offer the next best thing. Just say the word, and I'll make that trip home with you. Jeannie can find someone else to work the photo shoot. Hell, I wouldn't even care *what* they did about it. I'd hop in the car and ride with you at any cost. If you want me to."

Though she was normally an indecisive person, she gave a rather quick response.

"Frank, you're a precious man for offering, but I need to face this alone. I have some soul searching to do. This will change me forever, and I have much to put into perspective now."

"Rose, I can help you. I'll do the driving for you. I'll be there for you. I'll bring you coffee, or soda, or whatever you want. I'll sit up and talk to you. You can cry on me, or curse at me, or anything you need to do. Please, Rose."

But then he stopped. Frank knew if he said much more his feelings would be even more obvious than they already appeared. This wasn't the time to allow them to surface.

But he couldn't help himself. This wonderful woman was in front of him, and she was in pain. He took her face in his hands, and wiped her tears away from both eyes with his thumbs. She looked down to the left and the right, at each of his hands touching her cheeks. Just then, he lifted her head ever so slightly, and sweetly kissed her lips.

Those lips he had been looking at the entire time they had worked together. The lips from which he had fought so hard to keep himself away. He had watched them from across the conference room table, while she drank her coffee and chewed her gum and answered questions. He had waited so long to touch those lips with his own. And now he hated himself for letting his feelings out at a time like this. When he parted his lips from hers, he looked down in disappointment. But, to his relief, Rose looked up and smiled at him. It was the first time she had smiled since she received the phone call.

## CHAPTER TWO

After the kiss, Rose looked deep into his eyes. "Frank…"

"Yes, Rose?"

She took a moment to speak, but she didn't seem upset, so Frank took that as a good sign. Still, he felt he had been inappropriate. "I'm sorry, Rose." Frank turned to hide his face from her. All she could see was his wavy reddish blonde hair.

"Frank, please turn around."

He feared the worst, that she regretted his kiss. But he turned to face her once again and prayed she'd enjoyed it as much as he had.

"Did you kiss me because you felt sorry for me, or because you wanted to? I mean, is it something you've thought about before now?"

"I love our friendship, Rose, and our working relationship. I have all the respect in the world for you."

"Frank. The kiss…"

"Alright. Truth is, I've wanted to kiss you long before today, on many occasions. I confess. Seeing you like this made me want to fix everything for you. It wasn't that I thought a kiss from me would accomplish that, but I wanted to comfort you somehow. I felt your hurt, too. Not as deeply as you, but well, before I go on, does that make any sense? And I'm sorry if it adds to your decision to decline my offer of accompanying you to the funeral."

"Oh Frank, the kiss has nothing to do with my decision to go home alone. Truly, going alone is something I need to do. I hope you understand. And as far as the kiss goes…" and she stopped mid-sentence, leaving him hanging breathlessly.

"Yes, Rose?"

"The kiss was wonderful. I had absolutely no idea you felt that way. And, we'll talk more about it when I get back in a few days."

She simply didn't have room for it in her head right now. She embraced him and, as they separated, she tenderly kissed one of his hands.

"Will you help me close things down here in my office and then walk me to my car?"

"Of course, my dear. Anything you need. Let me know when you're ready to leave."

Frank stepped out and Rose sat alone in her office. It wasn't a presidential suite, but quite a nice office for a twenty-eight year old single woman. She looked around at all the objects which represented where she was in life. Her Bachelor of Arts degree hung on the wall, alongside various other recognitions and awards for her photography work. In the decade since high school, Rose had done well for herself.

And she still had a bright future ahead. After all, she wasn't even thirty. But Lily Harwell would never get a chance to have a bright future. It seemed so unfair. Why was Lily gone and she was still here? She didn't have time to think about all that though. She had to pack a suitcase and then drive the next day. Neither of which she wanted to do.

She shut down her computer and tidied up her office. She looked back once more at the frames on the wall. Why had things worked out so well for her and not for Lily? She picked up her purse and her laptop and, as she left the office, Rose realized how lucky she was. Maybe, just maybe, when she came back to work, she wouldn't hate those staff meetings quite so much anymore. At least she was alive to put up with them.

She messaged Frank that she was ready to leave the office. As she raised the blinds to the hallway and opened her office door, her coworkers tried to resume a busy look, though she knew they had been listening and waiting to see her. They all felt so sorry for her that morning. The group was more like family than colleagues, and she gladly accepted hugs and well wishes for safe travels from them all as she made her way out of the office.

Frank quickly appeared to walk Rose to her car. He looked into her eyes, still fearful he might have ruined things earlier with the kiss. But Rose gave him a look of approval which assured him all was well in their little world together.

He opened doors for her as they exited the office. Just as he pushed the elevator button, Jeannie ran back out to catch her.

"Rose, I'm so glad I caught you before you left. Just one more hug."

Although Frank considered Rose *his* closest friend, he knew she had a close relationship with Jeannie as well.

"Thank you, Jeannie. I don't know what I would do without you guys."

They both smiled back at Rose and reassured her this would all be okay, and that they would be waiting there for her when she returned.

"One more thing, Rose. Take as much time as you want. Don't feel pressured to return on Monday if you need more time. Visit around your hometown, sleep late for a few days or whatever it takes for you to deal with this. But make no mistake, you *will* be missed." Jeannie leaned over to whisper in Rose's ear, "You know Frank's at his best when you work with him, so please hurry back."

Rose laughed and looked at Frank from the corner of her eye.

The elevator door opened and Frank held it as she stepped inside. They both waved to Jeannie as the elevator doors slowly closed.

"Thanks for letting me walk you out," Frank told her as the elevator descended. Rose rested her head on his shoulder while they stood alone in the enclosed space. He leaned down and kissed the top of her head and smelled her fragrant blond hair. As the elevator doors opened, they walked out, and he kept one hand on the lower part of her back. Partially because he knew she had been weeping and was faint, and partially because he loved the way it felt. Suddenly, it became clear to Rose how much Frank had been holding back.

Why had she never seen it before? As sad as she felt right now, she also felt stupid. This thoughtful man who shared her love of photography had feelings for her. She felt a fool for being so clueless. Lily always had guys falling all over her, but never Rose.

Frank helped her into her car and reached in to hug her, still feeling awkward for the kiss he had surprised her with earlier. But he was surprised himself when Rose made a move to kiss *him* this time. It was only a small kiss, but the fact that Rose initiated it told Frank she was interested.

"You know, if you'd like to come back to my place, I could probably use some help packing."

She felt like she had pulled some sort of trigger, but she couldn't help herself. She wanted and needed his company that evening.

"Great. I'll order a pizza when we get to your place. That way, I know you'll get at least a few bites to eat, even if I have to force feed you," Frank said, with a little wink.

She rather liked the way that sounded. And she almost felt bad for exploring her feelings for Frank to any degree during such a horrible time. Rose had never been one to take advantage of a situation. But she felt good with Frank. She always had. And they had always functioned as a couple, but only in a work capacity. Or that's the way she had always seen it. Surely she hadn't been the object of anyone's silent affections. Or had she?

They arrived at her apartment. It was times like this when she was glad she hadn't yet opted for a house and a yard like many of her friends. She wanted all that, one day. But she also wanted someone to share it all with, and to share the responsibility of it. Rose was at a place in her life where it was all about *her*. And that was fine, because she had worked tirelessly to get there. Now was the time to do everything she wanted. She didn't want to look back on her life one day with regret, bemoaning all the things she hadn't done while she still had the chance. For now, she came and went as she pleased. But one day, it could all be turned upside down completely. And though she told no one, she honestly hoped it would. One day.

As they walked in the door, Frank placed her laptop on her kitchen table and took out his cell phone from his pants pocket.

"I'm ordering a pizza with the works for us. Okay, Rose?"

"Sure, Frank. Thanks a bunch. I really appreciate it."

While Frank ordered the pizza, Rose opened her laptop and logged in to look at hotel possibilities for the trip. Ironically, her favorite hotel in her hometown was near the lake where Lily had perished. But, she loved the hotel and had few opportunities to go there. Rose felt treating herself to a nice hotel, even in the midst of all this turmoil, was certainly permissible. One way or another, she would end up driving across the lake or near the old bridge. It was unavoidable, so she might as well be in her favorite hotel. When she had completed the reservation, she went into her bedroom and only partially closed the door. She slipped out of the beige pantsuit she had worn to work that day and into a comfortable red cotton summer dress. She also kicked off her sandals and decided to go barefoot for the rest of the evening.

She peeked out at Frank in the next room. He sat there patiently on her sofa, looking at a magazine, or newspaper, or something. Anything. Waiting on her. She walked into the room and up to where he was sitting. They didn't touch, or speak. They only looked into each other's eyes.

Finally, he put his hand on her back, moved it lower, and then even lower. When he reached the hem of her dress, he slowly ran his hand up under it, and all the way up the back of her leg. Not once did he look like he would stop, and not once did Rose consider asking him to.

"You're not wearing any underwear?" he asked her, as if it were the most serious question in the world.

Before she could answer him back, she saw his face light up.

"Oh, you're wearing a thong." It didn't really surprise him. Rose might have been a shy gal at times, but he always knew she was quite sensual.

"Yeah, I always wear thongs."

She continued to stand above him. And he kept his hand under her dress, firmly holding on to her hip. She moved a little closer to him, and spread her legs slightly so his knee was between them. The

13

tension was obvious, and the only noise in the room was the sound of their breathing. It wasn't long before he stood up and put his hands on her arms, still keeping her at a slight distance so he could take it all in. He looked her up and down, and up and down again. She heard his breathing grow heavier with each passing second. A few hours ago, Rose had no idea how he felt. Now, she was sure she was driving him crazy. And she adored the way it felt, and how he adored her.

Rose reached under her hair where the dress was tied around her neck. She slowly untied it, pulled it over her head, and dramatically tossed it to the floor. It was one of her favorite dresses but, at this particular moment, it was merely a piece of fabric interfering with a moment of passion.

He began to remove his shirt, and then his pants. As someone with limited sexual experience and a photographer of mostly women, she had never had many chances to stare at a fully naked man. She felt silly for being inexperienced, but this was no time to exhibit any insecurities.

She slipped off her thong. She took his hands and led him to her bedroom and onto the bed, never taking her eyes off him. Rose was suddenly glad she had remained on birth control pills, despite the fact she couldn't even remember when the last time was she had had sex. It had been at least nine or ten months, if not longer, and she almost breathed a sigh of relief as he lay down on top of her. Frank's completely unclothed body felt amazing. He kissed her lips, and her neck. It felt *so* good when he kissed her neck. He moved back to kiss her lips, and then back to the other side of her neck. It was almost as though he was starving. But then again, so was she.

And speaking of starving, her doorbell rang.

"Damn! The pizza. Don't you dare move," Frank said, as he stood up, put his pants back on, grabbed his wallet, and ran for the front door.

Rose put her hands over her face, embarrassed over the timing of things. They had altogether forgotten the pizza order. She listened to the transaction taking place at the door. She assumed Frank had hurriedly tipped the young delivery driver quite well when she heard, "Wow, thanks Mister!" It made her smile.

He slammed the apartment door shut, threw the pizza box on the kitchen table, and ran into the bedroom trying to shed his pants as he made his way back to Rose. But Frank lost his balance and fell on the bed with one foot stuck inside the leg of his pants. They both laughed for a moment, but were also a little worried the interruption might have changed the outcome of things.

But the laughing quickly turned serious again. As he made his way back on top of her, they reminded each other exactly where they were before the interruption. They kissed each other's mouths and necks, and then he slowly moved his kisses down a few inches at a time until she found herself clenching his back and pulling his hair. They surprised each other at their lack of awkwardness for a first time together. They were so completely in sync, as though their moves in the bedroom were a continuation of their already established friendship and work relationship. Rose didn't know where any of this was headed, but she only wanted to think about what was happening right now.

His tongue felt so good, and she loved how much attention he gave to every detail of her body. It was almost as though someone had given him the manual to her before he got started. It was uncanny how he knew what she would enjoy, and she had to wonder if him being ten years older than herself was helpful to the amount of pleasure he was giving her. When he knew Rose had been completely satisfied, he moved back up her body and gently kissed her face. Rose complimented him over and over on his techniques, and just when she didn't think she could feel any better, he put himself inside her. Each thrust felt better than the last. She loved the way they connected – body, mind and soul.

Rose didn't often act on a whim, but she felt differently about being with Frank. Working, talking, and traveling with someone for three years isn't exactly moving quickly. She looked him directly in his eyes. If she was going to bed with him after all this time, she wasn't about to close her eyes while it was happening. She wanted to live it wide awake, every single second it was taking place. And that's exactly what she did.

She loved looking up at his face as he finished, and hearing the sound of gratitude in his voice. It was all so personal, and they had revealed a side of each other they hadn't yet known, even after all the time they'd spent together. He looked so exhausted, and yet so exhilarated. She gently took his face in her hands and kissed his lips over and over and told him how wonderful it was. It was all so spontaneous and unrehearsed. And perfect. After her last kiss, Frank moved over to lie down beside her and pulled her up next to his body. She lay there in his arms, and it felt so comforting.

"Well now."

"Well now, what?" Frank replied, with a smirk on his face.

"Well now. I'm not sure what came over me. I don't normally sleep with someone so suddenly. I guess I felt like I had to say that to you."

"My dear, first of all, I wasn't here to judge you. I came back here to help you and--"

"Oh, you *helped* me," she assured him. "You helped me a lot."

"Oh, I did? You liked?"

"I liked very much."

She leaned up to kiss him again, then nestled her head back on his shoulder. It was as though she fit there perfectly, and yet she didn't quite know where to go with it all. She laid her hand on his stomach, and he rested his hand on top of hers. He touched each of her fingers individually, as though touching them for the first time.

"So, do you still want to talk about that kiss when you get back?" Frank asked, lost in her sweetness. She was sweet, and not because she was ten years younger. But because she was a purely wonderful creature who was interesting and deep and lovely. He adored her.

"Well, now I think we'll end up talking about more than just the kiss when I get back." She was afraid to let him know exactly how much she had enjoyed the time with him. "I did really need someone to help me tonight, but that's not why I wanted you to make love to me."

"I hope I didn't force myself on you or anything, dear. You have so much in your head right now and I didn't know all this would happen. I wouldn't hurt you for anything, I was only here to help you."

"I believe I came on to you once you got here. I could have told you to leave at any time if I had felt uncomfortable. Maybe I'm the one who came on too strong."

"Nope. Not too strong for me. Nope. Not at all."

Rose laughed and began to wonder what would happen now. She had her friend's funeral to attend and she had seduced her coworker in her bedroom while a pizza was getting cold in her kitchen. Was this really her life? And what about seeing him back at the office, fully clothed and working side by side again? Damn. She should have thought of that sooner.

"You're thinking of how things will be back at the office when you return, aren't you?" He could tell exactly what she was thinking by the contorted facial expressions she had unconsciously made.

"Well, a little, I guess. I mean, I lost my friend today, and here I am in bed with my work partner. I think that officially makes me some kind of tart or something, doesn't it?"

"Silly girl, of course it doesn't! You allowed me to comfort you, and I'm glad. And whatever happens with all this is fine with me. If you come back and we find out it doesn't work, then we'll deal with that later. If you come back and things *do* work out between us, then we'll deal with that as well. So what if we went in backwards order? We had sex first and maybe we'll start dating later. Some people start dating and think maybe they'll have sex later. Right?"

"Well, I guess. But I've never done things this way."

"And that's one of the things I've always liked about you. You're a bit reserved, and yet a bit unconventional and liberal at the same time. You're talented and fun. It's not like I tried to take you to bed on our first day of working together. This took a long time to happen. So don't torture yourself about it all. Okay? No matter where you and I end up, this doesn't have to be a negative experience. If we don't work out, then you can look at me one day on a shoot somewhere and think, *Yeah, I saw him naked.*"

Rose laughed again. As usual, she was over thinking everything. It was a flaw she had often tried to shed without success.

"You know, Rose, I seem to have worked up an appetite. I don't know why, but I'm starving all of a sudden. Do you happen to have any pizza lying around your place?"

And they realized that, once again, they had forgotten about the pizza.

They ate, laughed and talked like they always had, and drank a couple of beers together. And although it was only a little after seven o'clock in the evening, she felt exhausted.

"Well, now that we've devoured the pizza, do you actually want me to help you pack? Or have I *helped* you enough already?"

"I think maybe I've got it from here. But you've certainly been a *big* help to me."

The sexual innuendos could have gone on, but they both knew Rose had things to do.

"I'll miss you at work, dear. Will you at least text me occasionally while you're gone to let me know you're doing well?"

Frank hugged her a little longer and a little tighter than usual, but Rose didn't mind. It was fitting somehow.

"I'll miss you, too. And of course I'll text you. I had already planned on it."

They had one last very sweet *Goldilocks kiss*, as Rose liked to call them. Not too passionate, not too friendly, but just right. And so they finally parted, and she waved goodbye to him as he walked to his car and drove away.

## CHAPTER THREE

Rose still faced packing for her journey, but by now all she could think about was her afternoon of lovemaking. She hadn't let Frank know how special it was to her, though she certainly let herself dwell on it after he left. She looked up to the ceiling of her apartment as if talking to Lily, *How in the world can I talk to you about this with if you're not around anymore?*

She had never in her life imagined a day like this with so much sadness and laughter and sex all rolled into one. At least the myriad of emotions reminded her she was still alive. She had truly lived this day, and felt loved by so many. Of the millions of emotions in the world, she had touched on at least hundreds today. Maybe more. And now she realized how tired she was. So Rose lay across her bed, full from the pizza and beer, exhausted from crying, and comforted from the lovemaking. She decided to take a brief nap.

When she awoke, it was six in the morning. So much for her brief nap, but the sleep was an answer to prayer after yesterday. And yet, she had another long day ahead of her today.

She began to throw clothes she wasn't sure about into a suitcase she didn't want to pack, to travel to a place she didn't want to go. None of it seemed fair to Rose, but her best friend had just died, and it had changed everything. As a photographer, she had taken pictures of some of the prettiest and best dressed women in the world. While she continued to throw random articles of clothing into the suitcase, she hoped and prayed her own clothes matched, or at least weren't in total contrast of one another. Even thinking of matching clothes at a time like this seemed an impossible task.

She had packed too much in the suitcase, especially for the length of her stay. But that was nothing new to Rose. It had happened on every trip for the magazine, and Frank had always laughed at her for it. She sat on the suitcase until it finally shut, zipped it, stood it up and rolled it to the car. And she also made certain to take an umbrella because, unfortunately, there was a chance of rain. It wasn't that she hated rain, but it somehow made sad things sadder. How she hoped it wouldn't rain at Lily's funeral. It would already be sad enough.

The drive home probably wouldn't last more than four hours, but it would still feel long to Rose. As always, she knew music would help pass the time. Rose contemplated what music would be fitting for a drive back home to bury her friend. She wasn't sure, but she'd know it when she heard it, so she set her car stereo to shuffle through her music collection. At random, a modern version of *Auld Lang Syne* from one of her holiday music collections began to play.

She knew most of the world commonly associated the song with New Year's Eve celebrations, where everyone watches one year end and another begin. As a lover of poetry though, Rose knew the lyrics were originally a poem written by Robert Burns in the late 1700's. She also knew the song was used at many other occasions and ceremonies. Including funerals. It referred to old times past or days gone by and toasting to them with friends. She listened closely to the lyrics as the song played, "we'll take a cup of kindness yet for auld lang syne," and hummed its tune through her streaming tears. She cried so hard she could barely see the road, yet she continued to drive. Her days with Lily were now those days gone by.

The next time Rose had a *cup of kindness*, as the lyrics had so eloquently referred to an alcoholic drink, it would be in memory of Lily. And that toast would most likely be alone, back at the hotel after her visit to the funeral home. In fact, she felt so low, she thought she would need more than one cup of kindness to help her through the evening. And that probably wasn't anything she wanted anyone else to witness, despite the lyrics of the song about sharing that cup with friends.

As she entered the city limits of her hometown, she saw many familiar landmarks. The town had progressed little since she was born there almost three decades ago. And with her career and the larger city lifestyle she had grown accustomed to, Rose knew she could never live there again. Still, it was nice to return on occasion, only not this particular occasion. Rose drove over the new bridge on her way to the hotel. In fact, the new bridge and the hotel were some of the only notable changes her hometown had experienced. But her trip across the water only made her realize that Lily had no real reason to drive on that old bridge. Hardly anyone drove on it anymore since the new one had been built. It seemed as though she really had driven off it intentionally.

Rose attempted to mentally digest it all as she arrived at the hotel and walked inside with her luggage to check in. The stately ceilings and faint sounds of classical music playing overhead were a wonderful momentary diversion, and she was grateful to have something so lovely to focus on for a while. Rose took her room key from the hotel clerk. She grasped her hand around the handle of her rolling suitcase and made her way up to the top floor to her room.

The hall was long and winding, but at last she found her numbers on the wall beside her door. Her door, and her room, at least for the next two days. She walked inside, opened her luggage, and then stepped out onto the balcony to enjoy the view. The scenery was lovely, and after her emotional drive to town, the moments she spent high above the rest of the world felt like a mini-vacation. But, unfortunately, it had to come to an abrupt ending. It was now time to make her way to Lily's wake.

## CHAPTER FOUR

As Rose arrived at the funeral home, she finally felt the inevitability of it all. The people she would face, the facts she would be forced to accept. She parked the car and unfastened her seatbelt, almost in slow motion. She honestly hoped she would wake from a bad dream and wouldn't need to really walk inside the building after all. As much as she wished and hoped for life to be different right then, it wasn't. And so she reluctantly exited her car, took a deep breath, and walked inside.

Friends from school immediately noticed her, and gathered at the door to greet her, including Allison who had called her with the news. There were people who seemed glad to see her, but had no idea what to say to her. Everyone knew Lily's death would be painful for Rose. People used to call them the flower girls - Rose and Lily. It was always the two of them. Now it was just Rose. All on her own.

They hadn't been *as* close in recent years, but there was a bond between them that surpassed whatever time and miles they spent apart. And now they were even farther apart.

She did her best to hold back tears when she saw the spray of flowers on the casket. There were literally dozens of pink Stargazer lilies. It was still impossible to accept that her friend was inside there. She wasn't sure if she was upset or relieved when she realized it was a closed casket visitation. Perhaps both. If Rose had seen Lily's sweet face, not smiling, eyes shut, never to open again, she probably couldn't have handled it. She was glad the choice had been made for her.

Rose recognized Lily's father, and her sister, Lila, neither of which she knew very well. But they knew who Rose was, and thanked her for all she had meant to Lily during her short life.

"Well, I only wish I could have done more toward the end," Rose told Lila sadly, "but I had no idea it was near *the end*."

"My dear, she spoke of you constantly, even the last time I talked to her a few days ago," her father told Rose.

"I hadn't seen her in a few weeks or kept in touch with her as much as I should have. I mean, we all get so tangled up in our own lives, and we don't realize how precious it is until it's over." Rose bit her lip to keep from crying.

Lila leaned over and whispered to Rose, "I know you loved her. She told me you still loaned her money and helped her. I know you two still had a special friendship. Rose, she lived knowing you loved her. And she died knowing you loved her. Trust me."

While Lila's words were meant to be of comfort to Rose, they were small consolation to her now. Despite their sincerity, Rose walked away from them all still feeling empty because none of their words would ever bring Lily back.

Rose pulled herself together long enough to say hello to a few more people with whom she had attended high school. But she was here for Lily, and the small talk had simply gotten too small. Rose had been brave and strong on the outside for hours, but inside she felt like a weakling. She held her head low and, mostly hidden by tissues, hurriedly excused herself out the double front doors of the old funeral home and into the evening air.

It was warm outside, but a gentle breeze came in from the lake and blew through the trees which surrounded the parking lot. Yes, the same lake she had grown up loving, the same lake where her friend lived her last moments. She looked at it from a distance and tried to understand it all, but it was still too much for her to understand. It was too much for anyone to understand. All she knew was the evening air felt good on her face, which was flush from crying. She didn't want to go back inside to the restroom and see anyone else or explain any more tears. She didn't want to talk about where she lived now, or her career, or why she had ever left their sweet little town and why she could never come back there again. She couldn't deal with one more thing.

She turned her back to all the cars and opened her eyes wide so the sweet breeze of the evening would dry her tears. She hoped not too many people had noticed how much her mascara was running, or how hoarse she was from crying, or how crumpled her clothes were from the car ride into town. She felt a perfect mess, and wanted to hide from everyone. She had survived the public appearance but now she desperately wanted to run away. She wiped her face on a tissue one more time, took a deep breath, and looked up again. And there he was. Trevor Barton was standing right in front of her.

She remembered Trevor from high school, although she didn't know him personally. But everyone knew who he was because his father owned a store in town. She remembered him as outgoing, friendly, and adorably attractive. Ten years later, none of that had changed.

She had heard through gossip since she arrived that he was engaged to be married. Of course, she had heard a lot of gossip that evening, but she was pretty sure this much was true. And though it had been ten years since they graduated high school, it appeared as though high school would *always* be high school.

Knowing she was the friend closest to Lily, Trevor reached down and embraced her. She wondered for a minute if he had her confused with someone else. Maybe she had changed so much he had mistaken her for a different classmate. Maybe he had no idea who she even was at all.

"I was just headed out, Rose," Trevor said as he hugged her.

Well, he apparently knew who she was.

"I saw you inside and wanted to say hello before you left. I couldn't believe it when I heard the news. I know you must be devastated. I'm really sorry for your loss. You know, my dad and Lily's dad are close friends. That's another reason I'm here tonight. And my dad will be a pallbearer tomorrow. Anyhow, I didn't know for certain if you would be staying in town for the funeral, and I didn't know when I'd see you again if you weren't, so I wanted to speak to you while I had the chance. It's good to see you, and you look great. Life is obviously agreeing with you."

In the rambling but endearing way he addressed her, he both welcomed her back home again, and comforted her for her loss. Yes, *her* loss. Lily's family had lost a daughter, a sister, a cousin, etc. But Rose had lost someone, too. Her best friend. And Trevor was the first person who recognized her feelings in the crowd of others who claimed a loss. Rose thanked him and tried to make the kind of small talk she had avoided all evening but felt obligated to do now. She assumed he had merely been nice to her on his way out.

But, wait a minute. Did he just say he went out of his way to find her and speak to her? And did he imply she looked good? She was surely delusional from all the tears and must have imagined things far beyond proper perspective.

"Are you okay? Do you have somewhere to stay? Do you need a ride somewhere? You look really upset."

"Thank you, Trevor. And yes, I have somewhere to stay. I love the place over by the lake, so I got a room there."

He looked off to the side, and she knew what he was thinking.

"Yes, I know. That's near where Lily crashed, but I love that hotel. Maybe I'll be fine there, maybe I won't. If I can't take it, I'll find somewhere else to stay. But thank you for being concerned."

She reached out and took his left hand as she spoke and, though he wasn't wearing a wedding band, she recalled hearing the gossip regarding his engagement.

"So, I understand congratulations are in order for you." Rose slowly and reluctantly let go of his hand.

"Why? Oh, the engagement, you mean."

"Well, yes. That's what I meant."

Rose gathered something wasn't quite right with his reply. It also surprised her when he failed to mention that his wedding would take place in a couple of months. But she didn't ask. If she had to come back to town to bury her dear friend, at least being chased out into the parking lot by Trevor Barton wasn't the worst way to end the evening. Rose never really attracted the popular guys from high school. That was Lily's job. But the years since Rose had left her hometown had been good to her. And she was beautiful in her own way. Not in the bodily perfection, beauty pageant way Lily was, but easy on the eyes, thoughtful and pensive nonetheless. Not to mention a very talented photographer.

Indeed, she was pensive about the idea that, at this particular moment, Trevor stood directly in front of her. And he was in no hurry to leave. Knowing Lily would be laid to rest the next day, and that her life had been cut short, Rose entertained the idea of taking a chance on this moment. After all, she was only one flower girl traveling through life now, on her own. She no longer had Lily to make her smile and laugh and encourage her to take chances.

She allowed her mind to wander even more. If Lily were here right now, what would she do? What would her sweet, sweet friend Lily do? There was yesterday with Frank, and now with Trevor. She felt like she was walking through life with Lily's man-magnet capabilities. In fact, there wasn't a second where Rose doubted Lily was somewhere out there orchestrating it all. Wouldn't it be funny if Rose wasn't actually on her own? Maybe Lily was her guardian angel, steering all the men in her direction.

"Rose, are you in there?" Trevor said, touching her head lightly and pretending to knock as if to check for a sign of existence inside her.

"Yeah, I'm here. I guess since driving into town, I've grown a bit weary. Sorry, dear."

"Hey, don't apologize. I was just checking on you."

Trevor touched her shoulder with a level of familiarity which they didn't actually share. Rose began to wonder why he had followed her out into the parking lot. Was she actually being pursued by someone from high school the night before she buried her best friend? She took a moment to pull her thoughts together.

"Rose, I hope this isn't out of line, and I don't mean any disrespect whatsoever, but would you like to go have a drink? I know I could use one right now, and I'm sure you could, too. My treat, if you like."

"I don't know. It's been a long day."

In the same breath, she clenched her teeth at the idea she might have possibly conveyed an answer of *no* to him.

"Hey, I understand. Really. I figured maybe I shouldn't have even said anything to you. As a matter of fact, I should have asked first if you were here with someone."

"No, it's fine. It's only me," Rose said, holding up her left hand and waving her ring finger, free of any wedding or engagement rings. "Only me." But perhaps because of Trevor's offer, she wouldn't have to drink that cup of kindness alone after all.

"Well, how about we go to the restaurant at the hotel where you're staying? I'd at least feel better about making sure you get where you're going for the night. I mean, I know you're a hot shot photographer and all now," Trevor said, waving his hands back and forth in the air like she was a big deal, "but still, I'm just trying to be a gentleman."

She looked back up at him. He was at least a foot taller than her. She had forgotten how tall he was, or maybe she'd never actually stood close enough to him to know in the first place. Still, she couldn't help but focus on the severe difference in their heights.

"You think I'm a hot shot photographer, huh?" Rose said, mimicking the hand gesture Trevor had made when he said it to her a few moments ago. She laughed and thought it sounded just as silly when *she* said it. Though she didn't dare allow him to realize the intensity of what she was feeling at his mere presence.

"So, what's the verdict?"

"Well, I suppose one drink wouldn't hurt anything. Right?"

"Absolutely. We'll drink a toast to Lily. I mean, if that's okay with you. But I don't believe she would protest."

"You know, I think Lily would enjoy the idea of two people from her high school who both cared for her toasting in her memory. It's a wonderful idea."

He walked with her to her car, and even bent down into the driver's side across her body to make certain her seatbelt was fastened. Rose was certain it was an excuse to be close to her, but when she felt his cheek brush next to hers the attraction was immediate. And mutual. She waited as he walked to his own car and sat down inside. Rose released her car from the park position and moved toward the parking lot exit. But Trevor was only as far as her rearview mirror, following her each and every turn until they arrived at the hotel.

## CHAPTER FIVE

Once at the hotel, Trevor parked his car close to where Rose had parked hers. He walked over to her car to meet her, and they walked inside the hotel together. Not arm in arm, or even touching, but *together* still, somehow. It was almost more emotional than she had ever felt towards a man, even men she had known much better. She wasn't even well-acquainted with Trevor. It felt so juvenile, but walking beside him equaled some sort of religious experience. She was glad no one asked her to describe the feeling because she was at a complete loss for words.

Rose walked beside him as though she had known him forever, and intimately. He opened doors, and she waited on him to do so. They made their way across the lovely well-appointed hotel lobby, and it amazed her at the grace and ease with which they did it all. She had never known a feeling quite like this.

When they approached the hotel bar, he asked for a table for two and gave his last name to the hostess for the reservation. His unexpected company was most welcome at this bleak point in her life, and most especially on this particular dreary night she had assumed she would endure alone.

They were seated at a table for two, and they each ordered a beer. The waitress asked Rose if she wanted a menu and, though she hadn't eaten a bite all day, she didn't feel hungry. As she and Trevor drank together, they talked. About everything, and nothing. About important things, and not so important things. About food, and drinks, and places they had been, and things they had done. They spoke of dreams they'd had, and whether or not they'd ever come true.

They also talked of people they had lost along the way. He didn't have the eloquent words to express himself which Rose was accustomed to hearing, but it didn't matter. He had all the sincerity which could ever be heard in the voice of a friend left behind. And Rose was that friend left behind now that Lily was gone. When she paused, she felt the tears coming once again and tried to discreetly wipe them from her eyes. But they didn't go unnoticed by her companion for the evening.

"Do you need a tissue, Rose? I'm so sorry. I know this must be hard for you."

He always tried to make everyone believe he was a jerk. But tonight, with only the two of them there, he was far from acting like a jerk. In fact, he had been on his best behavior. But Rose didn't care about any of that. Tonight, she was having drinks with Trevor Barton.

"It's okay, Trevor. I still have so many more tears to cry. But how about that toast to Lily you promised me?"

Poor Rose was still fighting back other tears that were sure to fall, if not now, then tomorrow and in the days to come. She explained to him how she had listened to *Auld Lang Syne* on the way to town, and what it really meant, and how she was raising a cup of kindness to Lily that evening. She might have lost Trevor a bit since he wasn't a poetry and flowers kind of guy. Still, he understood the general idea and he listened to her every word intently, so Rose was pleased all the same.

Trevor raised his glass and, as if they had rehearsed it, Rose raised her glass to tap his. She held it there as he spoke.

"To Lily. She's absent at our table, but present in our hearts."

"To Lily."

His toast was much more eloquent than she had expected. He kept his glass next to hers and through her teary eyes, she could barely see his face. Still, she swore he had tears of his own.

"To Lily," Rose agreed again to the beautifully worded toast Trevor had made. She took a long and well-deserved drink of the beer, sat her glass down once again, and complimented him on his toast.

"Wow, that was lovely."

"Yeah, well, I'm not *always* a jerk."

They both laughed and took another long drink. In part to ease their pain from the loss of their friend, and in part to ease their nerves of being in one another's presence.

Finally, Trevor realized with the combination of Rose's long drive to town and her mental exhaustion over the loss of her friend, the alcohol had hit her rather quickly. Not to mention she had refused food for the evening. She drank out of regret and longing to have her friend back, and out of nerves from being with this attractive man. When the waitress came back to ask if they needed anything else, Trevor firmly said, "No," but with a grin, and paid the tab. As the waitress told them good night, a very late good night as it was well after midnight now, he began to walk Rose to her room.

He walked with his arm around her, through the long and winding hall, and made sure she arrived back to her room safely. It was a lovely hotel, and though she had been there before, it was Trevor's first time. It was a lovely place, even on such a sad occasion. So there they were, and Rose was a bit beyond her drinking limit. He took her card key, opened the door to her room, and walked her inside. He knew she needed sleep after such a long day, but that was far from all Rose wanted.

Sweet innocent Rose from high school, who never ever went *all the way* with a guy, pulled Trevor down to the bed on top of her and began to kiss him madly. It's not as if Trevor hadn't been imagining himself with her all evening. He had thought about it for hours, but had desperately tried to respect Rose and her emotions. Everyone knew Rose was a rather reserved girl in school, but she was a woman now. And though she still didn't have a great deal of sexual experience, she knew what she wanted. And right now, she wanted to continue kissing Trevor. She wasn't anywhere near done with him yet.

They rolled back and forth across the bed as they kissed, with the kind of kisses that made them both gasp for breath yet beg for more.

Trevor made her feel things she had only heard about. Right at this moment, innocent little Rose felt like the naughtiest girl in the whole world. She had her entire self to give to this man, and she needed him to make love to her. As she struggled for air to breathe, she made the decision to lose herself in him. She accepted every kiss, welcomed every embrace, and allowed her body to melt into his, completely lost in where she stopped and where he began.

Everything was new, and so exciting, and yet familiar. All she knew was that with every touch, she wanted more. And more. She moved her hands around his body as though she already knew him, as though he already belonged to her. They touched without awkwardness, and kissed without mistakes. They let their guards down and revealed sides of themselves to one another that only experienced lovers know. She felt so at ease with him, so comfortable, and so lustful.

After tossing around and around on the bed, she rolled him over on his back, and straddled his waist. He only looked moderately surprised, and certainly didn't complain, though she had never known a man to complain about a woman on top. He helped her off with her shirt, and her bra, and gently placed his hands on her warm, soft breasts. Rose unbuttoned his shirt, spread it open, and wrapped herself around him as she leaned down to kiss his lips. His hands felt marvelous against her skin, and she began to feel not so alone for the first time since she had arrived back in her hometown.

He rolled her over on her back, and got back on top of her again, still kissing her deeply and passionately. He then stood up for a moment and Rose prayed he wasn't stopping or, heaven forbid, leaving. But he merely wanted to remove the remainder of his clothes. Good heavens, Trevor Barton was standing in front of her completely naked. He leaned over the bed and looked at her skirt, the only article of clothing left on at this point.

"Now, how do we get this thing off?"

She anxiously sat up on her knees on the bed and grabbed his face again with her hands. She didn't want to take another breath without being physically connected to him somehow. As they continued to kiss, she pulled her skirt down to her knees, and Trevor laid her back on the bed and pulled the skirt, and her tiny lace thong, completely away from her body.

Rose felt how excited he was, and she reached for him. She held him in her hand for a moment, and loved how ready he was to be with her. He slowly lowered himself onto her and though she had been drinking, she was still very aware of what was taking place with Trevor. And she thought every second of it was amazing.

This really wasn't her style, yesterday with Frank, and now going to bed with Trevor without knowing him very well. But circumstances were all very different tonight, and logic had gone out the window. They rolled around on the bed, over and over, and Rose found herself back on top again.

She rocked her hips back and forth, and he held on tightly to her, passionately digging his fingers into her just a little, but not hurting her. She leaned over him and braced her hands on his shoulders as she looked straight into his eyes. She wasn't afraid to know who this man was, and she wasn't afraid to show him who she could be. Rose could hardly believe she was doing this, in this bed, in this room, in this hotel, and with this man.

When he was finished, he shook not only her body on top of his, but the entire bed. The way he sounded when he screamed, the pleasure in his eyes, the look of exhaustion on his face as though he had been awake for days. Yes, Rose was responsible for all of it. She wasn't exactly a take charge kind of gal, and certainly not in the bedroom. But this made her confident in a way she had never known. She liked being in control. She liked taking responsibility for what she got and how she got it. She wondered if other women had been doing this for years while she, hardworking little Rose, was still figuring it all out. Why had she never realized the pleasure she was capable of giving men? Well, this changed everything. But Rose couldn't contemplate it all that evening. She had invested so much in the lovemaking, as well as the cups of kindness earlier, and fell asleep only minutes afterwards.

Trevor relished the experience with her, even more than he had anticipated. And though she didn't find out until the next morning, he had gently kissed every inch of her naked body after she fell asleep. He had looked at her beautiful curves, her belly button, her face, her toes, and he couldn't help himself but to find out how she tasted. He knew right then that one night with her would never be enough.

As he continued admiring her, he wondered what would come of this night. He wanted more. He *needed* more. More of Rose and her body, but also of her heart and soul. He found her desirable in every way and wondered what it would be like to wake up next to her again. And when he had kissed each part of her body at least once, leaving out nothing, he put his head back on the pillow, and positioned her head in his arms. She was still in his arms the next morning.

When they awoke, Rose looked over at Trevor and smiled. He smiled back at her with a sly grin. It only made them want each other more, and have more of each other they did. He moved on top of her, sweetly sucked her breasts, and anxiously put himself inside her again. And it was as wonderful as she remembered. It felt right somehow, even though this was not the reason she had come to town. She could feel his excitement building, and the air was so full of the heat between them. They were communicating without saying a word. It was so fulfilling and complete. And when it was over, Rose began to cry.

"Rose, honey, what is it? Are you okay? Did I do something wrong?" He took her face in his hands and waited hopelessly for her to speak.

"No, no, not at all."

She took one of her hands off his back to wipe a tear from her face as it ran down her cheek. She missed that tear, but there was another one close behind, and then even more.

"Rose, I feel so terrible. I was so caught up in you that I totally forgot what you have to do today. It was cruel of me to want to make love again this morning with the funeral in a few hours."

"No, don't apologize. I wanted you. I needed you."

He rolled over and laid down on his back, but reached over to still cuddle with her. She laid against his right shoulder, and he pulled her next to him, closer and closer with each passing second.

"I'd offer to hold you during the funeral too, Rose, but I have to work the store for my dad," Trevor said sadly. "And even if I *could* go, I couldn't hold you the way I would want to because of my fia--"

Rose placed two fingers over his lips to silence him. She knew he was about to say the word *fiancée*, but she didn't want to hear it. Not then, not while they were naked together, wrapped in the sheets. So he stopped, and she thanked him for his kind offer.

"I'd love nothing more than to feel your arms around me during her service, Trevor, or even to feel you near me at all. Really. But we both know it can't happen. It's okay though. I'll make it. I may not look strong, but I *really* am. I'm actually a tough gal."

"Oh, my dear, I never doubted that for one moment."

He laid there at a loss for words, looking at this beautiful woman with whom he had spent such a beautiful night, and he didn't like seeing her so sad.

"Do you want to meet up sometime later? How long will you be in town?"

"Trevor, it's okay. I need time to process all this. And I'm sorry for having a bit too much to drink last night. I was mourning Lily, but I was nervous about being with you, being back here in my hometown, and burying my sweet friend. I do hope you enjoyed being with me though."

Rose prayed deep down to the very bottom of her soul he felt the same way.

"You were wonderful to be with, Rose. I'd love to do it all again."

She knew how much she would enjoy it again also, but she couldn't think about it. She ached as she kissed him. What a lovely little vignette of tiny goodbye kisses, seemingly platonic, but with the restraint which said, *If only I had a little more time with you...*

But Rose knew it would be nearly impossible to schedule another time together. Something special had happened with this man though, and suddenly, Rose's simplistic life had become terribly complicated.

He embraced her one last time before he left. It was so bittersweet, like a hello and a goodbye, all wrapped up around the two of them.

She couldn't bear to watch him leave, so she bit her lip and turned toward the beautiful hotel windows. She refused to look back until she heard the door close. Then she knew he was gone, and she finally allowed herself to look at the door to accept it. And then the tears began to fall, again.

She walked to the balcony window of her room on the top floor, and noticed rain beginning to fall. Almost like a mist. It was the softest rain she had ever seen, though not as soft as the sweet kisses on her lips only moments before. It was such a quiet and gentle rain. Rose began to gather up the items from the past few hours of her life, which had somehow completely changed now. She only knew Trevor was gone, and she had no idea when, or if, she would see him again. Her arms felt so empty, and her skin a bit chilled now in his absence. She wrapped her arms around herself to remember his embrace, in case it never happened again.

But the touch of her own arms only made her sad. Sad she couldn't rewind time back a few minutes and say goodbye once more, as painful as that would be. And since she couldn't, she watched the rain fall instead. Oh how she wanted a rain to wash all over *her*. She needed a rain in her life. A rain of imagination and creativity, a rain of new beginnings and fresh starts, and a rain of so many other things. She needed a good kind of rain.

But Rose had hoped it wouldn't rain at the funeral. That was the sort of rain that made sad things sadder. *This* is the rain Rose had feared.

It wasn't quite time to check out of the hotel room yet. Rose looked at the bed, still warm from their sleep the night before, still warm from their lovemaking, and still warm from lying in each other's arms before and afterwards. She couldn't look at the bed any longer, though she didn't want to venture outside and face the world either. She didn't want to see people, or hear noise, or experience anything which would distort the sounds and images in her head from the night she just had. She didn't want to face the sad rain yet either, other than watching it from the balcony window. And she dreaded Lily's funeral.

Rose found herself avoiding the bed as if it were a stranger on the street, so she knew it was time to go. The longer she stayed, the more it would hurt. Rose had booked two nights, but she knew another night would seem so lonely and empty compared to last night. Why had her time with Trevor been so much more difficult to digest than her time with Frank?

Rose had a dreadfully long day ahead of her, and there was no way she could have imagined going back to her hometown to bury her friend would result in something so complex. Next to getting through the funeral, walking out of this room would be one of the most difficult things she would ever do. But life would go on. Her night with Trevor was over now. But somehow, a part of her would remain inside that room, inside his arms, tangled in those sheets.

Her bags were mostly packed, except for the clothes she had chosen to wear to the funeral. She moved everything else next to the door. Without her things lying around the room, and without him now, the room began to look as it did when she first walked in, before she and Trevor had made it their own.

Rose held a dress up to herself as she looked in the mirror, gauging what she might actually look like for the day, but she ended up focusing more on her face. This time with Trevor had somehow totally consumed her, and she wasn't sure how it had happened or what to do about it. She took the dress off the hanger, placed the hanger back in the closet, and pulled the dress over her head. She smoothed out the fabric with her hands like little irons and then looked in the mirror. She opted for very simple makeup, assuming it would all end up on a tissue within a short time anyhow. And she needed her hair away from her face, so she pulled it back into a fancy hair clip. It would work well, she thought, especially since it was raining. There was no one to see anymore, no one to impress, and she knew she must dress practically for the days' events. Rose knew Lily, who was always dressed impeccably, would understand.

She looked under the bed, in the drawers, behind the furniture...certain she was forgetting something, but she wasn't. It was only a feeble attempt to make the memory of it all last a little longer. She closed her eyes and started to float back, but she knew that would be far too dangerous right now. She gathered her suitcase, her purse, her sweet memories, and walked out of that room. She shut the door slowly and heard the same dreadful click from the door as when Trevor had left the room. Rose began to walk down the long and winding hall, into the elevator, and very soon, out of the hotel.

As the elevator doors opened to the hotel lobby, she didn't even bother to slow down. She sprinted out the large wooden double front doors on her way to the car, despite the heavier rain now. There were bellhops who could have assisted her, but she quickly passed them, as she often did. She was stubborn that way. Rose didn't want help, especially that morning. It would only make her feel as though she had to be nice or speak to someone, and she didn't have any words to share right then. She loaded her luggage, closed the door, and sat down in her car behind the steering wheel. The windshield was wet, and she began to cry again, which made things even blurrier. She had to keep moving, but she had cried *so* much the past two days. Why had she thought spending the night with Trevor would be a good idea? Why had she allowed this to happen in the middle of saying goodbye to her friend? She initially thought this whole experience might be something to help her move on, but it appeared to have only brought her to a grinding halt.

She drove away from the hotel, looking back at the majestic building in her rearview mirror, and watching it become smaller and smaller with distance. She tried not to cry any more, but to no avail. Too much was sad today and the rain was making it worse. She said goodbye to Trevor, whether forever or for now. She was on her way to say goodbye to Lily, forever. She would soon say hello again to Frank, but what would that be like? The thoughts of it all engulfed her and made her feel so tired, and yet the day was still so new.

## CHAPTER SIX

Rose arrived at the funeral home. Immediately, the sight of people in black, sobbing into tissues and onto each other's shoulders, was enough to make her want to run back out the door. Rose observed the various displays of sadness. It was all so damn depressing. She felt so lonely and wondered if she had done the right thing by telling Frank not to come there with her. And Trevor *couldn't* be there with her. Well, it was what it was, and she had made the decision to show up alone, and so she would handle things somehow, on her own.

"Rose," a voice from behind her said softly.

Rose turned around to see who was speaking to her. It was Lila, Lily's sister.

"Rose, I'm glad you stayed for the funeral. I know how it is to come in from out of town. You never know who only comes to the viewing because they don't want to attend the funeral. I knew you'd be different. Thank you so much for staying."

"I can't imagine myself having made any other decision," Rose told Lila, and embraced her for a few seconds.

"Rose, I talked it over with Dad last night, and we'd like you to sit with the family during the service. We could use the support of each other, I know. It's not a long service, Lily wouldn't have approved. And there's no organ music, no taped music, it's merely a short and upbeat service. Lily was beautiful, and we wanted her service to be the same way. Anyhow, we'd love it if you would join us in the front. It would be our honor."

Rose had imagined herself doing exactly the opposite, hiding in the back of the chapel and sitting alone. Maybe even leaving for the cemetery ahead of the others, opting not to ride in the limo or with the family, even if they offered. She had it all planned out in her head, every possible way of sequestering herself during the entire event. She would drive her own car, in the pouring rain, on that very grey day. She would stand at the cemetery, on her own, back away from where the others would park in the funeral procession. She would watch from a distance, like one of those mysterious movie characters in a black lace veil. Of course she would have no real reason to stay, and while the family was saying their last goodbyes, Rose would drive off, on her own. Yes, she had it all planned out. Or so she thought.

Rose snapped back from her own thoughts and looked back at Lila, who was still there in front of her waiting on an answer. As much as Rose wanted to go with her whole withdrawn plan, she smiled at Lila and said, "I'd love to. And it would be my honor. I think Lily would approve of us all pulling together today."

"Oh, thank you, dear." Lila said pointed out to Rose where the family would be sitting. "We're on the first two rows, ahead of where the pallbearers will be seated. It's a small chapel and it looks like we might have a large crowd here. If you need to, scrunch up to the person next to you. Okay?"

"Sure. Whatever you guys need me to do is fine." Rose sure had moved up a long way from her initial thoughts of sitting alone in the back of the chapel. She looked up toward the heavens again. *You knew I didn't want to sit with anyone. You think this is funny, don't you, Lily?*

Lila was pulled away by another friend who wanted to pay her respects, so Rose took it as an opportunity to scope out the area where the family would be seated. It looked like plenty of room to Rose. But she hoped the scrunching would apply to everyone else except her. She didn't feel like doing much that sad, rainy Saturday morning, the least of it being scrunching.

But there was barely enough room for the family, even in their reserved area. There was indeed a large crowd, and it looked like the scrunching business might happen after all.

Rose had chosen to sit by one of Lily's cousins, Rhonda, whom she had known from school. Of course, Lila would be seated next to her father, along with a couple of her grandparents. Rose and Rhonda were the last two to sit down, and they realized there simply wasn't enough room for everyone. The funeral director approached them and began to assess the situation.

"Would one or both of you mind moving one row behind to the pew with the pallbearers?" he said to Rose and Rhonda. "I'm so sorry. We're trying to make room for everyone. It's one of the largest services we've had here in a while."

Rose felt comfortable moving. She had only agreed to sit with the family as a favor to Lila anyhow. "I'll move back a row," she offered. "It's okay, Rhonda. You stay here with your sisters, I'll be fine."

"Are you sure you don't mind, sweetie?" It's awfully considerate of you."

"Not at all, dear," Rose said as she gave her a quick hug. The funeral home director looked relieved and placed his hand behind her back to escort her to the next row.

Rose was not bothered at all by the move. She had initially imagined herself sitting alone anyhow. There was actually a little space between her and the pallbearers, so all was well. But the rest of the chapel was packed out like a rock concert. She knew everyone would miss Lily, and it made her feel good to see such a crowd there. Even if it did force people to scrunch.

The funeral director appeared at her pew again and tapped Rose on the shoulder. Apparently someone else needed to sit on the row. What now? There was no more family and surely one of the pallbearers wasn't late.

Rose kept her eyes on the front of the chapel and moved her legs over to accommodate this additional person into the pew. She was desperately trying to stay focused on the first few words of the service, but was distracted by the gentleman who stepped carefully across her feet. The smell of his cologne, the familiarity of his mere presence. When she looked up, she saw Trevor.

Rose stared at him, her face contorted, and with complete bewilderment in her eyes. He leaned over and whispered to her, "My dad was supposed to be a pallbearer, but he was sick this morning. He asked me to take his place."

What a turn of events. She had missed the warmth of his body ever since their parting kiss that morning, before the rain began to fall. Now, she felt his warmth once again. So soon, and so unexpectedly.

"What are you doing up here with the family?" he whispered, as confused by the whole seating arrangement as she was.

"Lila asked me to sit with the family this morning, so I told her I would," Rose whispered back. At that moment she felt like they were talking in the middle of a high school lecture and might be sent to the principal's office. This certainly was interesting. And after the whole messy goodbye that morning, crying about how she couldn't possibly be seen sitting with him. Rose smiled at him, because it didn't make sense, and he smiled back, certainly for the same reason. Then Rose looked upward to the chapel ceiling during Lily's farewell service and wondered if, yet again, Lily had orchestrated some sort of heavenly intervention for Rose. It seemed that way to her, but it was simply too preposterous to explain to another human being.

They felt very fortunate that fate, or Lily, as Rose would believe, had put them together. Rose gently laid her sweater over her lap, and put her hands underneath. She always had a tendency to get cold in places, and right now her hands were freezing. She had been in and out of the rain all morning, and the air was far too cold for her. Rose tried to stay warm and pay attention to the service, without paying too much attention to Trevor, and suddenly it became one big juggling act. She finally felt her hands begin to warm, and she realized Trevor, who she thought looked like a dream come true in his suit and tie, had slipped one of his very warm hands underneath the sweater on her lap. He was able to not only transfer a bit of body heat, but also offer that much needed support they both thought would be impossible for him to give her. He clenched her soft fingers, much smaller and colder than his own. And thanks to her sweater, no one knew anything about any of it. He looked at her and smiled, time and time again. She had wondered how long it would be before she could see or touch him again, and now here he was, only hours after their painful goodbye.

"I missed you after I left this morning," Trevor leaned over and whispered in her ear. She surely felt she would be struck dead for hearing such a sexy comment - and liking it so much - in the middle of a funeral service for her very best friend. It felt so wrong. And yet so right.

She didn't respond out loud, but merely by looking into his eyes and moving her lips with the words, *I missed you, too.*

Two short days ago, Rose was in a much different place. Bored in a conference room, and hadn't had sex in months. Now she had been with two men in two days. And she was saying goodbye to her best friend. Was it wrong in the middle of this funeral service to think of all the kisses she had received in the past two days, and all the places where she had received them? Shame on her for thinking of all these naughty things, she thought to herself momentarily. But maybe it was all part of Lily's gift to her - to keep the funeral from being so painful for Rose. If that was the case, then never had anyone given her such a lovely gift.

The funeral was drawing to a close, and Rose realized her mind had wandered terribly during the service. She almost hadn't remembered a word anyone had said. She stared at the decorative box in the front of the room which held the remains of her best friend. Rose knew Lily had always struggled in life for happiness. She hoped Lily was happy now, but felt sad she had to find her peace in the world beyond this one.

The service ended, and Trevor began his exit with the other pallbearers. He touched her on the elbow before he left the pew. "I'll take good care of Lily," he told her. And finally, after crying over Trevor that morning, and thinking of so many other thoughts during the funeral service, Rose cried her first tear specifically for Lily that day.

She watched the pallbearers dodge the rain as they each picked up one of the handles to carry Lily's casket. They moved it gracefully into the hearse for her final ride on earth. Rose felt proud, and quite moved, that Trevor would be one of the last people to help carry Lily. She knew at that moment no matter what happened with Trevor in the future, that her time with him last night, her seat by him today during the service, and the sight of him carrying Lily's casket would always be remembered as one single experience. Now, she couldn't imagine things having happened any differently.

Rose wasn't sure who to ride with to the cemetery. Trevor was with the pallbearers, and the family limo was full. Maybe she really *did* need time alone with her thoughts, so she took out her umbrella and sheltered herself. She walked to her own car, got inside, started the engine, and moved it in line with the others for the procession to the cemetery. While waiting for the cars to begin moving, Rose checked her cell phone. She saw a message from Frank which had been sent in the past ten minutes or so, asking if she was okay and wondering why he hadn't heard from her. Good heavens, she had forgotten all about messaging him as she had promised before she left home. And what would she say to him? *Oh sorry, while at my friend's wake, I slept with a guy from high school I barely knew and I lost track of time…*

Well, that was *not* the response she wanted to send. She took advantage of the extra time in line for the funeral procession to message Frank about how difficult things had been and that she would check back with him soon. She added a follow-up text to thank him for checking on her. Rose felt her head might explode, as well as her heart, but that would have to wait. The procession finally started moving.

On the way to the burial site, Rose had hundreds of things to think about, but she only wanted to focus on Lily. She decided to talk out loud to her, as though she were right there in the car with her.

*So, is this what it was always like for you? Guys always chasing you and wanting you? Because this is certainly new to me. I used to wonder what it felt like to be you, so pretty and always having so much attention. I used to convince myself it probably wasn't all that grand, but was I ever wrong. This is amazing. I'm having the best time of my life. Well, except I'm talking to an empty seat, and I can't share any of it with you for real now. I miss you, Lily. I really, really miss you. And I'd trade all this attention I'm getting for one day back with you again here on earth. But I know that can't happen. If you really are my guardian angel now, and I believe you are, then just know I love you. I've loved you since the day we first met in first grade, and I need your help in the days to come.*

She had started crying again, and she was so engaged in her talk with Lily that she didn't realize she had arrived at the cemetery. She hadn't remembered anything about the drive there, except the monotonous sound of the windshield wipers, tossing the water back and forth away from the glass. The road inside the cemetery was winding and hilly, and there were many large trees which would certainly stand guard over her friend's final resting place. She pulled up behind the car in front of her, stopped, and parked. Rose stepped out, opened up her umbrella, closed her car door, and reached into her pocket for a tissue before walking over to Lily's grave site. When she wiped her eyes and finally looked up, the first thing she saw was Trevor. There he stood with the other pallbearers, in the rain, removing Lily's casket from the hearse. She watched as they carried Lily's casket toward the area underneath the canopy for the graveside service. She couldn't take her eyes off the two of them, Trevor and Lily. Her past was with Lily, and her present was with Trevor. And it was the last time they would all be in the same earthly space together.

Through a sea of umbrellas, she walked near the canopy for the graveside service, but stood slightly apart from the rest of the mourners. When Trevor was done with his duties as a pallbearer, he walked over and stood near Rose. It was still raining, and he had no umbrella. She motioned for him to share hers, and he happily joined her underneath it. They never spoke, and given the crowd present, and even more importantly his engagement status, they were discreet. The minister asked everyone to move in closer toward the family while he spoke. Trevor placed his hand in a gentlemanly way across Rose's back as they stepped forward together, still sharing the umbrella. When the minister gave the final closing prayer, he reached down and gently placed two of his fingers around two of Rose's fingers and held them there while he knew everyone's eyes were still closed. It might have been a little risky, Trevor thought, but he wanted to hold her, and that's as much of her as he could hold at that moment. As they locked their fingers during the prayer, they gave each other a quick glance and then closed their eyes again. They continued to squeeze their fingers together tightly, but lovingly.

As the graveside service ended, the crowd broke apart from one large group back into the separate groups in which they had arrived. Back with the families to which they belonged. And there stood Rose and Trevor. They hadn't come together, and they didn't belong to each other. She wondered how they would leave.

They both walked over to speak to Lila and her father.

"I'm so sorry my father couldn't make it today," Trevor told them. "He hasn't felt well lately and was quite ill this morning. Thank you for allowing me to take his place on such short notice."

"It's us who should be thanking you, young man. You did us a great favor. Please tell your father to give me a call when he's feeling better. I sure could use his good company right now over a cup or two of coffee."

"I'll tell him, sir. I'm sure he'll be calling you soon about that coffee, too," Trevor added.

Lila reached out to take Rose's hand. "Thank you so much for making the effort to come in from out of town and stay for both the wake last night as well as the service today. It really means so much and it shows me again how much you cared for Lily. Thank you for all you did for her. So, are you going back home yet?"

Rose looked at Trevor, who had stepped away and was making small talk with a few others. "I don't know for certain yet. Without Lily here now, I don't know how often I'll be coming back to visit," Rose sighed.

"I understand why you're saying that," Lila told her, "but your home will always be your home, and you can still come by to see us. And to visit Lily's grave as well. But remember, Rose, this is your home and you'll always be welcome here."

Rose glanced over to Trevor again, and he looked back at her and winked. "Yes, I do feel very welcome here," Rose agreed. "Very, *very* welcome."

Rose said her final goodbyes to the family, and began to walk away. But when she looked to the spot where she had last seen Trevor, he was no longer there. She looked all around and up and down the hill where cars were parked, but she didn't see him anywhere. She felt a bit of panic, a moment of regret, and a sudden sadness. In her frozen moment of wondering what to do, she felt the buzz of her cell phone. It was still on silent from the funeral and she realized she had missed several messages. There were two from Frank, asking her to please call him when the funeral was over. She felt bad for not getting back to Frank, but she knew he would be there when she got back to work. Trevor was a complete unknown as to where it all came from or where it all was going. She scrolled down and looked through her other messages, and there it was.

*"Rose, my fiancée arrived at the cemetery while you were talking to Lila. She wanted to surprise me by showing up after she got off work a little early. It cut me like a knife to walk away from you without saying anything, but I didn't know what else to do. I didn't want to bring her up to meet you with no notice, but I didn't want to leave you either. I had to get her out of there ... I was worried I couldn't hide the way I'd be looking at you in front of her. Can we meet later, please, if you're not leaving town yet?"*

And then another text came in from Trevor.

*"Rose, please, I really need to see you..."*

Well, color her confused. Both the men she had just slept with were texting her like crazy. Looking up at the sky again, Rose found herself begging Lily for help.

Still standing under her umbrella, Rose felt the occasional breeze blowing in from the lake as she had done so many times before. She closed her eyes for a moment and tried to lose herself in it. She wasn't crying like she had last night at the wake, but today was even more confusing. She didn't mean for any of this to happen. She only came into town to bury her friend, not to sleep with someone and certainly not to break up anyone's engagement.

Her life had been so tumultuous since the moment she first learned of Lily's passing. There was Frank, so kind to her, so sweet, and so loving. But Trevor had moved her soul in a way she couldn't explain. The sound of his voice made her stop whatever she was doing, and his touch made her feel like nothing she had ever known. He made her laugh and smile. He made her feel wanted. Desired *and* desirable. She was so excited to have seen him again this morning, and she felt so lucky to have had him next to her during the funeral. He filled all her senses so completely. And yet, she had only been in touch with him for twenty-four hours. Twenty-four hours that had changed her world.

Was it wrong of her to think all these things about Trevor after such a limited amount of time with him? He *had* asked someone else to marry him, but that was before Rose came back to town. At most, she could really only stay another day or two. She knew Jeannie would allow her to take all the time she needed from work, but she actually missed her job, her coworkers, and her office. And Frank, well, she missed him, too. At least a little, she admitted to herself.

Finally, Rose texted back to Trevor as her fingers trembled.

*"I checked out of the hotel because I thought I wouldn't see you again. I was about to drive back home or at least go somewhere else. What do you want to do?"*

And then she hit the send button, and waited.

She quickly got a text back from Trevor.

*"I'm still with her right now. I told her I had to work later since I took the morning off for the funeral unexpectedly. But I'd lie about anything right now to see you for even a handful of minutes tonight. Please, Rose."*

Rose felt dangerous at all the sneaking around she was causing him to do. She had never been part of such a thing. And it shocked her because it actually felt exciting. Boring, unassuming Rose was now the other woman, and she anxiously read his next message.

*"Too risky to go to my house. Can you get that room back at the hotel? Or wherever you want to go. If you only want to have dinner, that's fine too. I just want to see you. Whatever else happens is up to you. Around 7:00 this evening. You name the place."*

Rose began to think, and tried to come up with some reasonable solution in her mind. Well, yes, they could simply meet for dinner and talk. So why had her mind gone straight to the idea of that hotel bed again? She thought she was someone who always looked deeper inside people, for substance. So what would it be for Rose that night, sex or substance? Well, the decision was simple. She wanted both. Trevor did say it was up to *me*, she recalled with a grin.

Rather than continue texting, she thought her next plan of action should be just that - action. So she drove out to the hotel to book a room again. Rose thought it would be easier to go back in person rather than make the reservation over the phone. And anyhow, she needed time to call Frank. She was concerned she might have already come across as rude with the scant bit of messaging she had sent him. She thought a phone call would surprise him.

Rose called Frank's number and put it on speaker as she started her car. She drove away from the cemetery toward the hotel she had checked out from only a few hours ago still in tears. Rose had a smile on her face and, for the first time since she had arrived at the funeral home, she thought back to her time with Frank. How quickly it all faded away after she began talking with Trevor. She listened to two rings go by unanswered, and then a third. She kept driving, and smiled as she thought of ways to greet him when he answered the phone. But she wouldn't be using those cute little words she thought of because he didn't answer. Instead, it went to his voice mail. Well, it wasn't the first time that had happened. She had worked with him for three years, and she knew photographers couldn't always grab a phone when it rang. She decided to leave him a message.

"Frank. Hi, it's Rose. It's been so emotional, being here and seeing all these people from my past and saying goodbye to Lily. I've thought of you lots since I got here, and of our goodbye before I left. Sorry I haven't texted much, but I've been so swept away by all the events here. Give me a call, if you want, but at least know I'm okay and surviving, on my own. I may stay another day or two, I don't know for certain yet, but I look forward to seeing you when I get back. Maybe we'll have *pizza* again," she said with a giggle.

She didn't know if it was over the top to say *I miss you* so soon, so she didn't. In fact, she didn't know what else to say. It had seemed like such a good idea to call him when she called his number. His picture even came up for a minute on her cell phone screen, and she looked at him for the first time really. He was a very nice looking man. How had she not ever noticed? Maybe it was because she had diligently tried to remain professional since being hired by the magazine. She had fought against becoming romantically involved with anyone in the office. But, she looked at his picture again now. What sort of wall had she built around herself that she had never allowed Frank inside?

The reality was, when she left her hometown, she probably wouldn't ever see Trevor much again, if at all. But Frank would still be a part of her life, and she would still be working closely with him at the magazine. They had traveled on so many shoots together and sometimes shared hotel rooms but never, ever, had he made a move on her before. Rose and Frank had always maintained a beautiful but strictly platonic friendship, or so she had thought. Now all her mind kept thinking back on was how he ran his strong hand up her dress in a search for her undies, only to realize a thong was there. Wow, she had experienced some really good sex this week. And she truly did want to have *pizza* with him again.

Well, the phone call didn't play out like Rose thought it would. She had envisioned a nice chat with Frank on the way to the hotel, but since that didn't happen, it had at least given her mind a chance to wander and remember some lovely events. Now she arrived at the hotel where, only this morning, she had left hurriedly with tears streaming down her face.

## CHAPTER SEVEN

Rose looked up to the sky. Of course it stopped raining *now*, after the funeral was all over, she thought. She walked back into the hotel with her head held high, and approached the reception area in the stately lobby.

As one of the well-dressed employees walked up behind the desk, he said, "Ms. Millican, hello again."

She had no idea why he had remembered her name, other than because she had so recently checked out.

"You remembered my name?" she asked the hotel clerk.

"Yes ma'am. But I thought you checked out this morning. I know your original reservations were for two nights, but I was certain you had changed your plans this morning."

"Yes, that's correct. But it's been a very long day, and if it's not too awfully much trouble, I'd like to have the room back. *That* room, or any room. I just need a room. Yes, a room. Please," Rose rambled on.

The hotel clerk thought she sounded a bit flustered, but she was a rather seasoned traveler with all the perks and points which came with frequent hotel stays. They immediately worked to accommodate her and get her into a room quickly and efficiently.

"And will that be for one night or multiple nights?"

"I'm not completely certain." And she wasn't. She honestly didn't know what would happen.

"Let's say tonight is a definite yes, and anything after tonight is a, well, a definite maybe."

The hotel clerk couldn't help but laugh at her. "Ms. Millican, the room you checked out of this morning has been cleaned and is available again. Would you prefer the same room or another room? It's your choice."

Rose smiled as she remembered the activity in that room only hours before. The kisses, the two of them, so passionate and free of clothing or any inhibitions. "You know, that same room will be just fine, thank you."

She briefly closed her eyes and sighed at the memory of it all, and at the possibility that history might repeat itself there that night.

"If you have your bags with you now, I'll call and have someone help you up to your room with them."

But Rose was not interested. "I only have one bag, and I'll take care of it, but thank you so very much. You've already helped me more than you know."

Well, she got the *room* back. Would she get *Trevor* back? She had no way of knowing for sure, but she had taken a gamble. Now to text Trevor back and let him know what was going on.

As soon as she reached for her phone, she had a text waiting from him.

*"Rose, are you still in town? Hoping to see you soon. Please."*

Rose began to text him back when her phone rang. It was Frank returning her call.

"Hello," Rose said, a little excited it was Frank, but also a little nervous about getting back to Trevor.

"Rose, finally. There you are, dear. How are you holding up? I've been worried and thinking about you so much. I know you're a strong lady, but this was a daunting situation."

"I'm managing," Rose said, with a bit of guilt in her voice. "The funeral was rough today. I had thought about coming home, but I think I've decided to stay. With everything I've been through, I would love to lie down for a while, kick back with a beer, and not do any more driving right now."

"Well, I can't say I blame you. I'm sure you need some downtime."

If he only knew she already had, as Rose thought of the double meaning of *downtime*. She suddenly felt flush while she struggled to answer.

"I need to stay here at least one more night, maybe two. I honestly miss work, Frank. I really do. The people here are nice, and I love coming back home to visit, but I need to get back to my life and my career. I've had the occasional comment about how I need to move back home again, but I could never do it. My life is where I am now, at the magazine."

"Working with an old guy like me, right?"

"Oh please, you're not old, silly man. Besides, I was wondering how you felt about having dinner when I get back?"

"Um, by dinner, do you mean dinner out or dinner in? Like *pizza*, for example." And there was a moment of silence between the two of them. It seemed as though *pizza* had become some sort of code between them for sex, and she enjoyed it immensely. Rose flashed back to her apartment, and how easily they made love after all their time as friends. How intense and magical it had all felt.

"You know, Frank, I think it all sounds good. All of it. Dinner out, dinner in, *pizza*, being with you. I like it all."

Frank seemed quite pleased at her answer, though he had no idea of all the other things floating around in her head which caused her delayed response.

"You like it *all*? Really? Now that's what I wanted to hear from you, Rose. I know you've been through so much lately, but you sure sound like a lady who knows what she wants. That's very sexy. I'm looking forward to seeing you, dear. I hope it's soon. Listen, I've got to get back to work, but it was lovely hearing your voice."

"Thank you, Frank. It was lovely to hear your voice as well."

After they said their goodbyes, Rose hung up the phone and held it up next to her heart. Frank's voice sounded so firm, so sure of things. She had always enjoyed his company. Frank was a take-charge kind of guy and it made Rose feel secure in his presence. His age difference and additional time in the photography field was reassuring to Rose. She had always looked to him as a mentor in her job and had learned a great deal from him since they began working together. Now she realized his age and experience had become something Rose found sexy and attractive about him.

She remembered she had not finished the text to Trevor because of Frank's call. She quickly ran her fingers across the cell phone screen to send a message to him, letting him know she had checked into the same room at the same hotel as the night before. A few minutes went by and she heard nothing from Trevor. She walked back out to the balcony where she watched the rain fall that morning, and where she felt so cold without Trevor's presence once he had left. The rain had finally subsided, and she thought walking out to the balcony would give her a chance to look out over the lake. With all the emotion of the funeral, she hadn't felt like taking out her camera even once. In fact, she had been so focused on her job, she had forgone most of the casual photography she used to enjoy. Now, as she looked out over the lake and her hometown, she realized how much she'd been missing. Her personal enjoyment of it led her to that career in the first place. She should use her camera whenever and for whatever she wanted.

So Rose stepped back inside the room and picked up her camera. She carefully walked back outside to the balcony and looked through the lens. That was the way she truly saw life, through the camera lens. Everything made more sense to her with her camera. She took pictures of the hotel grounds and the lake in the distance. Rose stopped for a moment when she saw Trevor in the courtyard waving up to her. She was so excited, but rather than greeting him, she merely zoomed in and began to take picture after picture of him.

For the first time, she really *saw* Trevor. The real color of his hair, his summer tan which had begun to fade ever so slightly, it all seemed different through the lens of the camera. He waved up to her, and she kept the camera to her face, taking pictures as she waved back at him with her free hand. She saw him pick up his phone, hold it up in the air, and then put it back up to his ear. Right on cue, her cell phone rang, and she saw Trevor's sweet smile on her screen.

"Hey there, handsome. Fancy seeing you here."

"Do you mind if I come up there, or do you prefer I stay down here and let you keep taking pictures of me?"

"You can stay down there if you want to, but there's only so many ways I can violate you from this far up."

Rose could almost hear his breathing become more rapid. She loved being the woman who could excite him so much. She played it cool in front of him, but she ached inside to do the things they hadn't been able to do in public together earlier.

"I, um, I'll be right, um, *up*."

He was intrigued by her offer of violating him. If he could have climbed the balconies one at a time to get to her faster, he would have. But he opted for the old-fashioned way of walking through the front of the hotel and using the elevator. It was only a few moments until she heard the knock on her door.

As Rose opened the door, Trevor was already reaching inside to touch her. They embraced, and suddenly she felt his lips, and his tongue, and his whole mouth around hers. So many kisses as though they had been separated forever. Maybe in a way they had been, she thought.

He wrapped one arm behind her back and pulled her into him. Rose felt her back arching so much she thought she might fall backwards. But he kept pulling her in closer, and even closer up to him. She softly kissed his neck, and it only made her want more of him. All of him. They continued to kiss as they moved across the hotel room, feeling their way and peeking between kisses to find the surface of their next encounter.

He started to lay her back on the bed, but she resisted. He tried again, and she still wouldn't give in. Instead, she twisted him around to the smooth, polished desk. Rose felt sad right then that such a great piece of furniture was almost certainly used by all the other guests as a boring work space. Trevor looked confused as she pushed his back up to the desk, but he didn't dare stop her to ask her why.

Rose kissed him softly, over and over, and when he started to speak, she put one finger over his lips to silence him. She kissed his chest, opening one button of his shirt at a time as she kissed her way down to his waist. She ran her hands up under his open shirt and she watched his face, loving his complete appreciation of her right then.

Rose unfastened his belt and removed it from the loops of his pants. She held it up to him, doubled it, and made a snapping noise with it. Now she was certain she had his undivided attention, mental *and* physical. Then she laid the belt to the side and began to slowly open his pants. She pulled down his zipper and reached inside his boxers. She moved her hand all around from front to back, and she loved the way he felt...so tense, so excited. Rose wanted to be everything to him. She slowly began to lower his pants and boxers all the way to the floor, until they lay in a puddle around his ankles. She looked at him longingly. Trevor could neither speak nor move, excited for what might come next, and the fear it might stop altogether.

Rose kissed his lips, and then his chin, and she continued to move down to his chest, stomach, and below his waist. She could hear how excited he was with each breath he took, and she could certainly see how much he wanted her. She knelt down in front of him and looked back up into his eyes. She took him inside her mouth and wanted him to know just how much she enjoyed it. Rose knew it was a very special place to be, and she made that part of him her entire world for the next few minutes.

When she moved back up to embrace him, he took her face in his hands and kissed her so very deeply. He then took her shoulders and turned her around so she had *her* back to the desk now. He gently picked her up and sat her on the desk in front of him. Their faces were almost at the same level now, and he moved in closely to kiss her. Rose's heart was pounding as he pulled her dress up around her hips and moved her thong to one side with his finger. Before she could feel, or even think, they were one again. She didn't want it to end, but when it finally did, they embraced each other and said nothing.

Oh, how much trouble she'd gone to, Rose thought, to get back this beautiful room with a bed full of feather pillows and down blankets, when all they needed was a flat surface and some privacy. They laughed at how it had worked out, but they wouldn't have changed anything. And though the sex had felt fierce and even a little wild at moments, when it was all over, he delicately lifted Rose from the desk, and sweetly placed her back on the floor in front of him. He even helped smooth her dress back down, just as Rose had done that morning in front of the mirror before she left the hotel. They embraced innocently, and clung to each other, until Rose finally spoke.

"Whew."

Trevor laughed and kissed her forehead. Then her lips, but only a peck. "Did you say whew or wow?"

"Well, I think I said whew, but it also gets a wow."

"You thought it rated a wow?"

"Well, of course. A definite wow. With some wow left over even. You were great."

"Rose, you are so great to be with. And I hate to take a chance on ruining it all by asking this, but what do we do now?"

Rose wasn't sure where he was going with the conversation, but she took his hand and led him over to the bed and pulled down the covers. She took off her dress and laid it on the back of a chair and then lay down on the bed, patting the sheets for Trevor to join her there. He sat down beside her.

"I don't know, Trevor. What *does* happen now? I wasn't expecting any of this, and I'm not sure what it means to either of us."

All they knew was they felt so good when they were together. When they laid on the bed next to one another, it was perfect, even without sex. The warmth they shared was so incredible, and they played with each other's hands while they searched for the next words to say.

"How long can you stay tonight?"

"I told my fiancée I had to stay late at the store, and we would get together tomorrow evening for Sunday dinner instead. She knows my dad has been sick and that I've been covering the store. I don't think I can leave you tonight, Rose. I brought a bag in case you wanted me to sleep over. I have no idea what's happening either, but I know I can't break away from your arms tonight. Will you let me stay here all night? In your arms, or you in my arms, or something? I can't leave you right now. Maybe overnight some magical answer will come to

57

one or both of us. If we stay together tonight, maybe we can brainstorm on something that will work."

They both felt anxious with each passing second, and almost more worried about their time together coming to an end than anything else. They tried to take their minds off things by watching television. Then, Rose surprised him with a question.

"Do you love her, Trevor? Your fiancée, who you haven't once yet referred to by name in my presence. Do you love her?"

It was a question he wasn't able to answer with any certainty because he wasn't sure of the answer himself. He reached over on the bed covers for the remote and pressed the mute button.

"I've known Stephanie for a long time, Rose. Our families are friends and she's a really nice gal. We get along well and we both like a lot of the same things."

Trevor struggled for the right answer, but his choice of words didn't seem so impressive to Rose. It was unclear whether Trevor didn't love this woman, or if he didn't know what love was at all. Rose wanted with all her heart to believe what she had with Trevor was different. But they had only been together a couple of days. In the grand scheme of life, what was two days? They had no past, so was it feasible to believe they really had a future?

Trevor's cell phone rang, and when he looked down at the screen, he saw his fiancée's name. He looked at Rose and held up the phone as he walked away to take the call. She stayed out of the way, while he took calls from her, and while he checked in with work. She went out of her way to stay out of the way.

After the phone call, Rose reiterated her statement from earlier.

"Do you love her, Trevor? I'm not trying to trick you into saying anything, and I'm not looking for any particular answer. And I'm not waiting on you to say you want me instead of her. But you did ask her to marry you. I'm merely asking if you really love her. Does your heart ache when you're not with her? Do you think about her when you're not close to her? When you make love with her, is it like when *we* make love?"

"Rose, *please* stop with all the questions. Here's the bottom line. I have a lady who just isn't interested in the things you and I have enjoyed together physically. She's nice, but not adventurous or sexy. Not like you. But because of my family's business, I'll stay in this area. I just assumed I was destined to end up with someone from this area. Though I've only spent a short time with you, and most of it has been physical, I swear what I feel for you isn't just physical. I can't completely explain it, but I feel things after two days with you I haven't felt with Stephanie in all the time I've known her. I've never met a girl like you, Rose."

Trevor looked down sorrowfully, and kissed Rose's hand as though she were royalty.

She couldn't help herself around him, and everything she normally suppressed about herself she felt free to show him. He was good for her in that regard. All her inhibitions were gone and, with him, she threw caution to the wind. All else in life was forgotten. She adored his personality. It was a rather haphazard approach to life on occasion. But it was a lifestyle she had never been able to adapt for herself, and it was enjoyable to be near. Rose knew *she* could never live that way, but she was able to live it just a little when she was with him.

She craved him like water in the desert. She wanted to do everything with him, in every way, in every position, and as often as possible. And yet, as much as that all satisfied her, holding him without the confines of clothing, alone and free with no judging eyes staring at them, she feared it would still leave her empty somehow. If not immediately, then a short time later. Not in her mind or heart could she make sense of such a horrible feeling, but it was a feeling she could not shake.

Her insecurity about Trevor wasn't anything she wanted to ever discuss with anyone. Rose was, in fact, a tad embarrassed at the entire situation. She had never been one for casual sex, and no one knew what she had shared with him. At least she had been able to enjoy the sheer physical presence of a warm body near her while she processed Lily's absence.

"You know, Trevor, I don't have any answers, but I do know in a few hours we must part. So let's lie here together and try to get a little sleep before morning."

She nestled down beside him and tried to forget how impossible their situation seemed. He enjoyed how she stroked his stomach with her fingernails and lightly scratched his skin. Then he rolled over to lie on his stomach.

"You've done it now. You have to scratch my back, too."

So she began to scratch his back, and then she sat up to speak.

"Wait, I have another idea. If you'll let me."

"Honey, there's not much I would say no to you about," he said with a sexy little grin which Rose wanted to capture forever. And there was only one way to do that.

## CHAPTER EIGHT

"Let me take your picture. Please."

"You took plenty of me earlier, didn't you? You know, from the balcony when I got here. And then you made that remark about violating me and, well, I don't remember much afterwards because all the blood left my head. But I do remember you taking my picture, over and over."

"I know, but this is different."

"How so?"

"Well, I, I don't know quite how to word it to you."

"Tell me, babe. Just say it."

A small tear rolled down her face. It was an overflow of all the tears that had welled up in her eyes. Tears which would eventually fall, but she had restrained them up until now.

"We both know what happens after we leave this room is a complete unknown. It would be nice to sugarcoat it and say we'll meet at a certain day and time and that it will all be wonderful, but we can't. And I don't know if it will *ever* work out for us."

Trevor laid there silently, doing his best to continue eye contact with Rose. But he realized the truth in what she was saying. He kept touching her hands the entire time she spoke.

"What I do know is that we had an incredible couple of days together. I loved every minute of loving every inch of you. What I'd like to do, as a photographer, is capture that memory. You, right here, just as you are. I want to capture the look on your face. The look you have after our lovemaking. How relaxed you are. The smile on your face. The desire for me I still see in your eyes. Maybe if I take a few pictures of you like this right now, it will allow me, no matter what else happens in my life, to remember these days I had with you."

"That's really beautiful, Rose. The way you think is beautiful. You're this really great gal who is so pretty, and even the way your brain works is pretty."

Trevor fumbled a bit for the right words to express himself, but Rose knew exactly what he meant. It made her smile, and yet a few more tears still fell down her cheeks.

Trevor felt a tad self-conscious about having his picture taken the way Rose described it. And though he didn't feel at all as wonderful as she made him sound, he consented. Rose walked over to remove her camera from its protective bag. She lifted the camera as though it were part of some religious rite. And though she had taken thousands upon thousands of photographs in her life, this was the first time she ever truly felt a relationship like this with her camera. She turned it on and made some adjustments, and while still nude herself, began to photograph Trevor on the bed.

This wasn't her standard photo shoot. She didn't strategically position him, or use artificial lighting to create a certain effect. She merely took pictures of him the way he was. Capturing the moment was her only concern. It felt so spiritual to her, and there was a certain humility in the way she did it. By remaining nude herself, she exposed her own vulnerability. Rose was sometimes self-conscious about her own body, but she knew this was a way to show her appreciation to Trevor for allowing her to photograph him.

Rose took some pictures of his face, and his smile. Some from the side to get his profile. She wanted to remember each kiss from him, what his lips looked like, how many eyelashes he had, and other details that were certain to eventually fade from her memory as time passed. She moved all around him. Some photos she shot in sepia tone, some in black and white, and some in color. She knew no matter how far away from him she would ever be, for however long – maybe even forever – these pictures would always return her to this moment. They would forever capture what she felt would be one of the most special times of her life.

As she moved freely around the room, she caught a glimpse of something on the wall. She lowered the camera from her face and stopped taking pictures.

"Rose, are you okay? What is it?" Trevor knew something had emotionally shifted within her. He hadn't known her very well for very long, but still somehow he knew.

"I…just…noticed it. Right there…how have I missed it?" Rose said, as if answering no one in particular.

Trevor was a little perplexed and almost wondered if she had finally begun some kind of emotional meltdown. It wouldn't have surprised him, or anyone else for that matter. After all, she had been through some very difficult times the past few days. All in all, she had held up rather well, but this didn't make any sense to Trevor. He got up from the bed to look from her same angle. Then he saw it.

A gold-framed impressionistic style painting, like some kind of modern day Renoir, hung above the hotel bed. In the painting, there were two women talking at a table. Many people were in the background, but the main focus was the two women, and sitting on the table was a vase of lilies. And just like that, she lived the phone call from Allison all over again. She once again realized why she was back in her hometown, in this perfectly decorated hotel room with a perfect view of the lake, with a perfect stranger. And both of them were naked. None of it would have happened if Lily hadn't died. Somehow Rose had not yet noticed the vase of lilies in the painting. But it seemed so obvious to her now.

And so she confessed to Trevor she had felt Lily's spirit all along, all through being with him, and everything else that had happened since she learned of Lily's death. She told him about so many things in her life, but she never told him about Frank. No, she couldn't tell him about Frank.

Trevor pulled her close to him. So very close. He knew how it felt to love someone who was no longer alive. He was amazed at how deeply she felt things in life. He felt emotions too, but he didn't feel them like Rose. He had never experienced anyone like her before, and he was sure he never would again. He had been awakened to something new by being with her, and he would be forever changed because of it. And he kissed her ever so sweetly.

"Rose, what you were saying earlier, about wanting to capture a moment. Well, I'm no big time photographer like you are, and you may think this is ludicrous, but I'd love it if you'd let me take a couple of pictures of you. I mean, it would only be with my cell phone, but still. Because I always want to remember what *you* look like right at this moment."

He had begun to see Rose as a completely beautiful human being, in every way. And while he enjoyed her body sexually, he had for the first time in his thirty years learned what it was like to find a woman attractive in ways other than physical. Rose never replied, but her eyes gave him the permission he was looking for. He took out his cell phone, stepped back, and took two pictures of her from the shoulders up.

"You can take them of the rest of me too, if you want," Rose said, knowing what he was thinking, even if he didn't realize it himself.

"Really? You wouldn't mind? I mean, I adore the whole package, but if you don't mind…"

"If I minded, I wouldn't have offered. How do you want me?"

"All the time, sexy lady. That's how I want you."

Rose blushed a little. Not because she was nude in front of someone she barely knew, but because she had never had those sorts of words spoken to her. She walked over and sat down on the bed, and began to pose provocatively.

"Is this what you had in mind?"

Trevor was stunned. It was quite late, but he would happily lose an entire night's sleep in exchange for the continued company of this special lady.

"You're amazing," he said, with the smile of someone who had just won the lottery. He took a picture, and stood there in complete silence, obviously aroused by her sexuality.

Rose began to freely move around in various positions, allowing Trevor to make as many pictures as he wanted. She thought it was fair for him to have pictures of their time together, too. And most of all, as someone who was always behind the camera finding the beauty in others, she enjoyed the idea that someone found *her* worthy of being photographed, for a change. She actually found it exhilarating.

Finally, Trevor turned off his cell phone and placed it on the table next to the bed. He knelt down on the floor in front of her at the edge of the bed and moved his index finger in a *come hither* motion. She crawled across the bed to him and kissed him on the nose. She had never felt so playful, or attractive.

"I don't know how I can let you go home, Rose."

"Let's not talk about it right now."

By this time, it was three in the morning, and they had both been awake for over twenty-four hours. Up until then, they had both felt invigorated and brand new. Rose assumed it was the sheer adrenaline of enjoying one another before it was no longer an option. But it would hurt to say that out loud, so she kept it to herself. But finally, exhausted in every possible way – in her mind, her body, and most of all her soul, Rose yawned, and then Trevor yawned in turn. They snuggled in the bed under the covers, and Rose fell asleep. Trevor, however, lay awake and continued to look at her. He wondered about *everything* in his life now. He thought he already had things figured out. Then, at last, Trevor fell asleep. And so they lay in the silent solitude of their hotel room, and absorbed whatever they could from one another. Their bodies searched for the rest they needed, but that their minds refused to give them.

But as it does every day, morning came. No more excuses, no more postponing. They awoke and looked at each other, and knew they didn't have much longer together. Trevor had to get back to the store, and the time for goodbye was near. They knew words were futile, so neither spoke. Trevor knew tears were not a common occurrence for him, and he avoided them so not to upset Rose any further. It was their last lovemaking for now, for a while, maybe forever. There was no way to know.

He took her in his arms and held her, and he felt her warm tears drip down and roll across his shoulder. Too many tears to stop, too obvious that she cared enough *not* to stop. He kissed both of her eyes, and all the tears he could catch in time. He softly began to make love to her, and though Rose never actually stopped crying, she loved every moment. She tried to memorize exactly the way everything happened. The tender way he touched her, the way he felt inside of her. She had often heard of how two people could be one, and thought it was an overused and exaggerated statement. Now she finally understood.

When it was over, Trevor kissed her once more and without speaking, went to shower. Rose knew if she joined him it would merely start all over, and there was no time. She began to pack. Again. Her face was warm from all the tears, and ironically she wasn't sad about anything that had happened. She was only sad for not knowing what would happen next. She packed her suitcase, knowing she would not be returning another night this time.

Rose walked over to Trevor's black canvas travel bag, and looked at it as though it were mysterious. Rose was inquisitive, and though there wasn't much to learn from it, it was his. She envied that bag. *It would leave the hotel with him, and return home with him, unlike her.* She thought of leaving a note inside for him to find later, but she didn't want to appear nosy for having opened his bag. And what if his fiancée found it? That would be disastrous. She would never want to hurt him. So she ran her hand around the edge of the zipper, as though tracing it in her mind, just to feel something which belonged to him. And then she walked away.

When he stepped out of the shower, he said something silly and made her laugh. It was the first time they had spoken in a while. Yes, she thought. This is way I want to remember it all. The laugh, the smile on his face and, of course, the pictures.

"You can get in now, if you want to."

He looked so cute there with the towel around his waist, and his hair still damp, lightly dripping down his forehead.

"You know, I'm only three or four hours away, and I think I'll opt for a nice long bath when I get back home. I'd rather not rush before I leave here."

"Sure thing, baby. I was just offering."

He reached over and kissed Rose for no real reason except that he wanted to. Nothing fake or planned, just a sweet and lovely kiss. A

*Goldilocks kiss*. And as simple as it was, it was one of her favorite of their entire time together.

And while they had been together, the world was their own. Only them, touching one another in a way only people who had explored one another's bodies touch. Now they had to go their separate ways. Trevor would go back to his store, with his father. And to Stephanie. And Rose would go back to her job, with her camera. And to Frank.

She checked her phone and saw at least three messages from Frank. She didn't read them in their entirety, but she sent a quick reply so it didn't appear she was ignoring him. It was all she could do, knowing her time left with Trevor had come down to mere seconds. Everything about her belonged to Trevor right now. Anything she sent to Frank would be brief. But it needed to be kind and sincere since she would face him soon. Maybe even that evening.

And though she had enjoyed her time with Trevor, she probably didn't have a future with him. She needed to focus on her own life and keep an open mind to what might happen with Frank. Rose didn't know how she would feel about him once she saw him again, but he would most likely want to see her as soon as she returned to town. Her best approach would be to cry all the way home and get Trevor out of her system. And then, hopefully, she would have time to shower and change before Frank could get to her apartment.

Rose felt awful though. Frank was a truly quality person. And though she had only been with him one night, she felt as though she had cheated on him somehow. It was merely his unfortunate timing of becoming physically involved with her as just she got to know Trevor. It was all so confusing to her still. But that was something she could think about on the way home.

Now she was packed. And he was packed. And the moment she had dreaded since she agreed to have a beer with Trevor the night before Lily's funeral had finally come. They wheeled their luggage together towards the bedroom door. They both stopped to leave their card keys on the furniture near the television. But after Trevor turned his head to open the door for her, she reached back to grab her key as a souvenir of the stay. It might be all she ever had to tangibly remember it by. She made sure he didn't see it, and prayed he didn't have to go back in the room for anything, only to notice it wasn't there beside his. It would feel silly to explain to him why she had taken it.

They walked out the door, and they both cringed slightly when they saw it completely close and heard it latch. But they faced it all bravely as they looked at each other and wheeled their luggage down the long and winding hall toward the elevator.

Once in the lobby, the staff recognized her from her second check-in and looked over as though they might call her by name on her way out. But when they noticed the look of severity on her face, they merely made a nod with their heads and smiled. She did the same back to them.

Knowing anything she and Trevor did at this point would be painful, she looked at him as if to say, *Please don't make me say goodbye to you*, but it had to happen. Trevor walked Rose to her car, and placed her luggage inside for her. These two people in an unenviable situation embraced, having experienced a connection that some people never know. So while they were sad, they were also grateful. They continued to embrace like lovers, separated by war or years apart. But Trevor knew here in the parking lot, no embrace he engaged her in, no kiss he placed on her lips would be better than anything they had already experienced. But still, he took her face in his hands, and kissed her so, so gently. When their lips parted, he touched his forehead to hers, and they ran their hands once more up and down each other's arms, cherishing every part of their goodbye. He embraced her for the last time and squeezed her tightly. Then he placed his lips next to her ear.

"I love you, Rose."

She was somewhat surprised, but glad, because it gave her a chance to say what she felt as well.

"I love you too, Trevor."

They kissed each other's cheeks one last time, simultaneously. With hands still touching, they began walking away until they were too far apart to touch anymore. Rose turned her head quickly, and refused to look as he walked to his car. She jumped in her own car, started it, and left the parking lot. Watching each other leave or following each other on the road would be too painful. And so she left. She left the hotel where she fell in love with Trevor, she drove over the lake where her friend lost her life, she left the city limits of her hometown, and she headed back home, on her own. And while she drove, she cried.

And each mile she drove farther from Trevor seemed like thousands. For the first twenty miles or so, she felt as though she might not make it. Tears streaming down her face in between the smiles as she remembered him. Every touch they shared, every laugh they laughed, it was all the very best. She wouldn't be crying if it weren't so wonderful.

That's why she hated to keep driving. She thought of turning back, but it wouldn't solve anything. She shuffled the music on her car stereo, then tried scanning various radio stations. But no matter the song, station format, or musical genre, every song reminded her of Trevor. Which made her miss Lily all the more, because she couldn't talk to her about it. All she wanted now was to cry the rest of the way home, unpack, take a nice long shower, and try to decide what was next in her life.

She tried to drown out the sound of her own weeping with the music, yet somehow she still managed to hear the ring of her cell phone. She looked down, praying it wasn't Trevor because she wouldn't have the strength to say no to him. About anything. But it was Frank.

Rose did her best to clear her throat and blow her nose quickly before she spoke, but Frank was no fool. He didn't know *everything* she had been through, but he did know the sound of a woman who had been crying. She was in no shape to talk, and she tried to explain that to him, but Frank was concerned for her.

"Please Rose, listen. I want to stay with you tonight. I don't have to sleep in the bed with you. I'll sleep on your couch, in your floor, in the bathtub. I don't care. I only need to know you're okay. I can't bear for you to stay alone right now. You've been through too much. Please, let me take care of you."

There was a small part of her who wanted to tell him to go away, but she couldn't. She was merely upset right now, and none of it was his fault. He had been good to her in every conceivable way. She knew that he was worried and simply didn't want to see her suffer alone. She knew he cared for her now, and she felt badly about ignoring his attempts to contact her on the road the past couple of days.

"I'm so sorry I wasn't communicating well, Frank. It was one of the hardest times of my life, and I had to figure it out as I lived through it."

"Oh, baby. I'm really so sorry you had to go through this."

Never had she heard more sincerity in a man's voice. It was calm, and sure, and even peaceful. And they really were each other's best friends. It was especially true for Rose now that Lily was gone.

"Frank..."

"Yes, dear. Anything. What is it?"

"I don't know if I'll be good company tonight. I'm somewhere between falling asleep in the bath and throwing something up against a wall merely to hear it break. My emotions are all over the place. You really don't want to spend time with me. It wouldn't be fair to you at all."

Frank had worked all weekend to get ahead so he could take off some time with Rose when she returned to town. He knew she would still need time to recover.

"Rose, I told you a few days ago. I'll do or be whatever and whoever you need."

"Yes, you did Frank. You did. I'm warning you though. I'm really not good company."

"And I'm warning you. I don't care."

"You really don't scare easily, sir."

"Nope. So can I come over? Pretty please?"

"Okay, okay. You win. Come over. But I've been crying, I'm an emotional wreck, and I haven't had a shower. I don't even think I ate yesterday. I'm not fit to be around," she said, again doing her best to convince him not to bother, but to no avail.

## CHAPTER NINE

Frank grabbed a bag of clothes and necessities for an overnight stay at Rose's apartment and threw it in the car, almost literally. He stopped at the local market and selected all sorts of goodies from the bakery, three kinds of beer, and two different wines. He also chose some foods he had seen her eat before such as cheeses, breads, and other treats. He planned an entire picnic for her. If she didn't feel like being out of bed, he would bring everything to her in bed. By the time he packed his clothes, ran his errands, and drove to Rose's apartment, he pulled up next to Rose at exactly the same time.

She got out of the car, and stood there, looking at Frank. Her mouth said no words, but her face said, *Help me*.

Frank walked over to her slowly, picked up her purse and bag, and helped her into her apartment.

"I know you must be exhausted. Let's get you inside so you can rest."

He carried her luggage to her bedroom, and opened it over in a corner of her room but didn't unpack it. Then he walked to her bathroom and started running her water. "Did you want a bath or a shower, dear?"

Good heavens. He hadn't tried for a kiss or a hug or even a silly little grope, or anything. He had carried in her travel bags and never asked for anything in return. Obviously he cared for her, and he had made jokes about *pizza* since she had been gone. She knew he cared for her as a friend, and so much more, but he was slow and patient. That certainly was impressive. For anyone. Her mind was still in a fog from burying Lily and being with Trevor. But Frank had been a solid and constant fixture in her life for three years, and if nothing else, she needed to remind herself of that fact.

"I think I'd like a shower," Rose told Frank. She almost asked him to get in with her, but he said something about having things to bring in from his car. He was treating her like a princess already, she thought, but she had no idea what he was about to do.

Rose swore to herself when she left the hotel she would shower as soon as she got home. And when she said *shower* in her mind, that meant washing off the tears she cried, sadness for losing Lily, her heartbreak in leaving Trevor, and everything else from her trip. She needed a fresh start, and that shower would be the cleansing which allowed her a fresh reentry into the life she woke up to last Thursday morning.

As Rose prepared for her shower, she slipped out of the clothes she had been wearing – a soft white knee-length summer skirt, and a sheer aqua blue short sleeved shirt, with a keyhole cut in the front. She clutched them in her hands, and stared at them as though they were somehow magical. She placed them next to her face for a minute, and breathed in the all the scents from the fabrics. She could still smell Trevor's cologne. His embrace was absorbed in them. But they would have to be washed as well. Before she opened the hamper to add them to the rest of the dirty laundry, she clung to them one last time. Then she slowly and sadly dropped them in. Tearfully, she walked naked into the bathroom for her shower.

Rose didn't see him, but Frank had been quietly unpacking groceries in the kitchen and had walked by her bedroom to see if she needed anything. He had been a bit distracted by her lovely nude figure, but he also noticed she was holding the clothes near to her face. As a photographer, Frank had learned to read people's actions. He could see things from their soul that only reveal themselves to someone behind the lens of a camera. He knew her actions were indicative of something. And though he wasn't certain, he had a feeling it was because of someone other than Lily.

But Frank didn't mind, whatever it was. He was keenly aware Rose was a gal who felt things deeply. Frank was thirty-eight years old, and he had loved and been in love more than a few times in his life. In recent years though, especially since Rose had begun working with him, he had been rather withdrawn from the dating scene. It was partially because of focusing more on his career, but he would be lying if he said it didn't also have something to do with Rose. Besides, Frank never believed he was the only man in the world who found her desirable, and she had just visited her hometown. And she had made a point of going alone. Maybe it *was* all because of another man.

But really, none of that was important to him. He was allowing his mind to wander and it was interfering with his mission. He came to the apartment to help Rose and to give her a beautiful welcome home picnic. If she wanted him as her colleague, friend, lover, or some combination of things thereof, any and all of it was fine with Frank.

He tried to focus once again on the picnic. Frank spread out a blanket on the floor of Rose's bedroom. He placed the various foods he had purchased in a well-arranged fashion so it resembled some sort of movie scene. The assortment of appetizers, beverages, and desserts were ever so appealing. He only hoped that, no matter what Rose had been through, that she could still allow herself to enjoy the time they would spend together.

Rose didn't mean to spend so long in the shower, but the hot water felt so refreshing. It was just the sort of rain she needed. She finally felt better after washing away the tears and memories of the weekend. She heard Frank, moving around outside her door, but she didn't mind. He'd already seen her up close and personal, and she didn't have anything to physically hide from him. They'd seen each other at their very best and very worst while working together. Everything from dripping sweat on an outdoor summer photo shoot, to dressed in formals at award dinners.

Rose wasn't sure how to make her exit from the shower. She didn't want to imply anything by openly walking out naked, and she didn't feel any need to put on a robe, so she wrapped a towel around herself and stepped into her bedroom.

She was moved beyond words at the site of the picnic on her bedroom floor. She stared at it and walked around the four corners of the blanket Frank had placed so beautifully there. She was amazed and began to cry. She reached to put her arms around Frank in gratitude for his precious display. She felt a combination of water droplets. Some fell from her hair, still wet from the shower. Some fell from her eyes, as tears of joy. How nice to finally cry because she was happy.

She continued to embrace him and reflected on being in his arms only a few days ago. She had almost forgotten how sweet it felt…his arms, his friendship. As she moved to let go of Frank and walk over to the picnic, her towel fell. She had been using one of her hands to hold it up. She didn't care though, and she wasn't embarrassed, but she didn't mean for it to happen.

Frank reached down, picked up the towel, and handed it back to the naked lady in front of him.

"I believe this is yours, my dear."

She hadn't dismissed the memory of Trevor, but she needed to allow herself space from him. The drive home reminded her that he would most likely continue his engagement and go through with his impending marriage. It didn't change how she cared for him, but she also had concluded in her long steamy shower she must move forward with her own life. And right now, that included Frank, who was a complete gentleman.

Rose reached back for the towel Frank handed her.

"Oops."

She wrapped the towel back around her, loosely, and began to tell Frank what a beautiful job he had done.

"You did this for me?"

"Well, I figured I would help you eat a little of it. There's quite a bit of food here. I mean, if you don't mind sharing your picnic."

"Frank, of course you're staying. I don't know how much I can drink since I'm so tired and still have to make it back to work tomorrow."

"Rose, I hope you don't mind, but I took the liberty of talking to Jeannie today. She insisted that you not come back to work tomorrow. She found out you were driving back here the day after the funeral and felt you needed at least one more day of rest. She even gave me the day off too so I could keep you occupied and away from the office. And she said if I had to tie you up to make sure you didn't come back to work on Monday that I had her permission. Now Rose, do you *want* me to tie you up?"

"Well, so long as it's not too tight."

Rose looked at Frank with eyes that made him melt. He suddenly felt quite warm inside from the idea of thinking about tying up this lovely woman.

"Ahem," Frank said, as he cleared his throat.

Rose was still stunned at the picnic setup Frank had created for her, and so she continued to hold the towel around her chest as she kissed Frank on the cheek.

"You're so sweet for doing all this, Frank. Really. It's so lovely. I've never, ever had anyone do anything like this for me."

She kissed him on the cheek again, and he worked diligently to restrain himself. Rose kissed his other cheek, his lips, and then she dropped her towel. This time, on purpose.

"I'm guessing you don't want me to pick that up for you this time."

"You would be correct."

Naked, Rose held him a while, though he was still fully clothed. She didn't know where she wanted it to go, but she knew it felt good standing there with Frank's hands touching her skin once again.

"Rose, are you sure you're not hungry?"

"Why Frank, are you sure you're not trying to ignore me?"

"Certainly not, Rose. But I didn't want to seem like I was pushing myself on you after all you've been through. What happened before you left wasn't planned, and I didn't want you to think this was either. I wanted to take care of you. I didn't come here with the intention of going to bed with you, but I can't say that I don't want you, because I do. I do, shoot me. I want you so damn bad right now, Rose. But I swear, that's not why I'm here."

"I know, Frank. You've been my friend for three years apparently wanted me for a while and I was totally clueless. I have no idea why I didn't see it, but I didn't. When you made love to me last Thursday night, I could finally feel it - all the times you had restrained yourself, and simply been my friend. It's been there a while, hasn't it, Frank?"

"Of course it has. You know it has. Well, at least now you know. I might have kept it inside forever if it hadn't been for watching you hurt when you got that phone call last Thursday. I didn't mean to reveal such a personal side of myself to you in the middle of your loss, but I guess I couldn't help myself."

Rose turned her neck towards his lips as a hint to kiss her there. And he did. He wanted every single inch of her. And so he kissed, and kissed, and kissed a little more. Then he stopped and ran into the other room without a word.

Rose wondered what in the hell she had done. She thought things were going well, and she had no clue what she could possibly have done wrong. Finally, after Rose stood there naked in her own bedroom, seemingly abandoned by her would-be picnic date, Frank ran back to her bedroom door.

"Close your eyes," he yelled from the other side.

"What?"

"Close your eyes. It's a surprise."

"Good grief. Really?"

"Really. But I promise, it will be worth it."

When she opened her eyes, there was a lovely bouquet of six pink roses. It was beautiful, with a little string of pearls around the edge, like a necklace. Roses. For Rose.

"One is for Thursday, the first day we made love. One is for Friday, when you left town and I missed you so much. One is for Saturday, the day you had to bury your sweet friend. One is for today, the day you came home. One is for Monday, which we can spend together....away from work and from the rest of the world, if you like. And the last one is for Tuesday, when we'll go back to work to the jobs we both love, and figure out whoever we are in each other's lives. Whatever you decide is fine, but I'll always remember my few days of worrying about you and being with you, and that's what this bouquet is about."

In all her years of listening to men say words meant to move her, this was something she had never heard. It was so unique, she knew it had been conceived and tailored especially for her. It was an amazingly well-thought out concept. How very beautiful. Half a dozen days, explained as a gift, with half a dozen roses. This was something only derived from a beautiful man, both inside and out.

Rose hadn't dated all that many men, but she'd been out with enough to know that things like what Frank had just done for her didn't happen very often. She felt horrible for comparing Trevor and Frank. They both did things she loved. But she would be lying if she said she didn't still have Trevor in her head. She'd washed him off her body in the shower, she'd wash him out of her clothes in the laundry, and she'd cried him out of her life through her tears. But he was still inside her. And he might be forever, no matter who she finally surrendered her love to one day. It would be difficult to ever forget him and move on with her life. But if Frank were capable of things like the bouquet of flowers without being prompted, it certainly would make it easier to leave Trevor behind. Especially since he was already promised to someone else.

"Frank, I don't even know what to say. In fact, I'm speechless. How did you think of this?"

"Well, it's really quite simple. You, sweetheart, have made a mess out of my life ever since I met you, but especially for the last few days. I wouldn't change any of it mind you, but it is what it is."

Suddenly she felt like a bit of a tramp for moving back and forth between Trevor and Frank, but it wasn't as if she had planned any of it. Rose didn't play those sorts of games. Besides, who could plan days like these anyhow? These were far from ordinary days, and they certainly didn't come into her life frequently. Until this week, that is. She was almost afraid to go to sleep, wondering what madness tomorrow would bring.

"The roses are incredible."

Rose hugged him sweetly, and then kidnapped his neck for some nibbling. "You know what else is incredible, Frank?"

"Um, no. I really, I mean, well, you're incredible, Rose. I don't know much right now…"

"Frank." Rose stopped kissing him and took his face in her hands.

"I've had a difficult weekend. I can't go into all of it right now, but I want you to know that being with you the night I found out about Lily's death gave me a strength I'd never known. You lifted me up when I felt I might die. You took care of me and comforted me in a way I didn't know was possible. I can't explain it, but I know giving myself to you that night made me a better and stronger person to face this past weekend."

"Really? You mean that?"

"Of course I do, silly man. I don't say things I don't mean. And I don't play games. Well, not emotional games. I might be coerced by a man like you to play a few more games…"

"Rose, I guess at this point I don't have to tell you I'm hopelessly crazy about you. I'm sorry if it's too soon, but things have moved so quickly. You don't ever have to play a game with me as long as you live. I was in love with you the moment you walked into the magazine that first day."

Frank gushed as he began to unload years of feelings on her. She wasn't sure she was ready for it all, and honestly Frank had reservations as well. But he didn't want to keep sleeping with her without telling her how he really felt. It made her admire him even more at that moment. More than she ever had before.

"I'm kind of hungry…" Rose started, but was interrupted by Frank.

"Oh good, sweetie, I'm starving. Let's dig in. What do you want to start with first?"

Rose still stood there, naked.

"Um, sweetie, I was about to ask you to make love to me, and *then* we could have this fancy picnic. You don't have a problem with that, now do you?"

The woman didn't have to ask him more than once. He began to tickle her and chased her to the bed. She begged him to stop, as she was quite ticklish, but by then they were on the bed together. He went from silly to serious, and ripped his own clothes off in record time to get closer to her.

"Rose, are you sure you're okay with this?"

"Frank, please. Make love to me."

He was a bit old-fashioned, but she adored his years older than herself. He was one of those men who looked younger than his age, but he knew more, protected her, and made her feel safe. He cared for her as a friend, colleague, and lover.

Frank never said another word, and with fewer of the anxious moves that Trevor had, he slowly and lovingly made the next moves towards having her completely. She almost felt that he went too slowly, but she knew he was making the buildup more special. She loved that. In the short time she was away, she had made love with Trevor several times. She had only been with Frank once, but she loved his technique and his pace. Suddenly now, with Frank kissing every inch of her body and making his way towards being inside her, she felt Trevor's name and even the memory of his touch slip further and further from her existence. As much as she had cried over him in the past few hours, the realization of how a man like Frank felt about her meant a great deal right now.

Frank made slow, sweet love to her. It was a little less lusty than their first time together last Thursday. He kissed parts of her he had unintentionally missed the last time, but still gave her all the attention, as well as the thrill, from before. Rose loved the difference between the two times, knowing the same man could make love to her in such different ways only days apart. Maybe she was realizing how he had helped her, or maybe she was thinking about all the wonderful things he had said to her since she returned. But she knew she was under the spell of this man now who, up until a few days ago, was simply her fellow photographer at work. Heaven help her for not being aware of all that existed right under her nose, or the way he could make her feel in bed.

They both lay there after their loving, exhausted and more than satisfied in every possible way. They laughed and talked for a few minutes. But suddenly, Rose had an appetite. And a feeling the picnic would be devoured.

They sat on the bedroom floor together, enjoyed the food, and celebrated the picnic as though they were together in a grassy country meadow. While Rose sampled a little of everything from the picnic

Frank had so lovingly prepared, she stopped long enough to lean over and kiss him. She felt stupid, because she still had a mouthful of food, but she only puckered up enough to give him a closed-mouth kiss. She may have thought it was silly, but it meant a great deal to Frank.

"You know, Frank, why is it whenever you're done making love to me, I feel famished? It's like, I can't get enough to eat. I mean, last time I practically fought you for a pizza. And look at me tonight. It's a good thing you brought enough food for an army because I think I may eat it all. I do believe, sir, you must wear me out completely."

"And you make me crazy, my dear. I can't help but devour you when we're alone. As hungry as you are right now for this picnic, well, that's how hungry I've been for you for three years now."

"Sweetie, if I knew you could make me feel like this, I wouldn't have left you this hungry for this long."

They took a moment to enjoy the private picnic and all the interesting things they were learning about each other. Physical and otherwise. They felt lucky to have discovered such a great relationship together. After they had eaten much of the picnic food, some of the wine, a couple of beers, and even a bit of dessert, they decided to turn on the television.

Frank insisted on cleaning up the food while Rose got ready for bed. He stored the leftovers and then joined her under the covers a few minutes later. He pulled her close, they watched television, and even remarked how they shared favorite shows and networks. They sank into the bed and enjoyed the warmth from one another's bodies. It was all still so new, but his body felt so familiar to her already. Even the conversation felt familiar, almost like home to Rose. She looked up to the ceiling, waiting to hear if Lily had another message for her. She sure could use her to talk to right about now.

"Is there something on the ceiling I missed?"

"No, I just sometimes feel Lily around me. When I think of her, I look up. Or when I want her to send me a message. I suppose you think I'm a total kook now, huh?"

"I think it's fine. Don't ever think anything you do is crazy to me, Rose. I have my own weird hang-ups and quirks. Certainly you've been witness to those from working with me for this length of time. If you can connect to Lily in *any* way now, after she's dead, then you must have had a really strong connection with her while she was still alive. I have no preconceived notions of how you should handle the death of someone, but I do want to say this to you."

He stopped, and leaned over towards her in bed, and lifted her chin with the side of his index finger.

"I know you turned to me for comfort Thursday when you found out you lost her, but I believe it would have happened eventually anyhow. I don't believe you're in bed with me right now because you're trying to cope with something. It may have given things an extra push, but I think it would have ultimately happened regardless. Do you understand what I'm saying?"

"I do, Frank. I really do. And I'm glad you don't think I'm insane for talking to a dead woman. I miss Lily, and I never thought of what I would do without her. Maybe I'm only imagining her talking to me when I look up at the ceiling. Maybe it's only me wishing I hear something from her. We were always a pair, you know. Rose and Lily - the flower girls."

"That's sweet, Rose."

Frank repeated both their names aloud. "Rose. Lily. Both flowers. I hadn't put that together until you said it. You two were the kind of friends who didn't have to always be in constant contact to know what was happening with one another. Am I right?"

"Precisely. That's why I feel like, even though she's out there *somewhere* now, and I'm here, I know she's still with me. In a different way."

"I think it's a perfect explanation, Rose. In fact, I think almost everything about you is perfect."

Rose was getting sleepy, and she felt so very guilty when she heard Frank say those words to her. If only he knew what she had done while she was gone. Still, she had enjoyed a good thing with Frank before she left. And then she found another good thing with Trevor while she was gone. And she enjoyed that, too. But Rose was always somewhat of a tortured soul. Rose had some serious feelings to consider, and she would have to do it, on her own.

She kissed Frank deeply, and told him how much she appreciated all he had done to save her lately. From going crazy, from not eating, and even from herself. She honestly had no idea how she might have handled being in her apartment without him there. She was lucky to have him in her life.

For now though, she needed sleep. Sweet sleep to replenish her body and soul. The kind of sleep Frank was already enjoying as he lay next to her. It was her first time to share a bed with him all night. She wasn't sure if he was the snuggling type, but Rose thought it best not to disturb this wonderful man who had already done so much for her. So she laid beside him and slept. She even thought she might be falling in love with him. Just a little. But she said it out loud to no one. Yet.

## CHAPTER TEN

When she awoke the next morning, Frank was no longer in the bed, and Rose thought she heard voices. Voices which sounded like attempted whispers, but still loud enough to wake her. She pulled back the covers, got out of bed, and slowly started to walk out of the room. Then she remembered she was naked. In case there was actually another person nearby, she grabbed a robe before leaving the room. She didn't usually use a robe, but she had one handy for reasons such as this.

When she stepped out of the bedroom, Jeannie was standing inside the front entrance to Rose's apartment talking to Frank. Rose started to walk out of the room as if she were at work, in her regular office clothes, and then she realized what she was about to do. By walking out in a robe, it would be clear they had slept together, and Jeannie was standing there in the middle of it all. Well, it was too late now. But Rose had always prided herself on being a modest person who didn't flaunt her personal business. Especially in front of business people.

"Morning, sunshine," Jeannie said to Rose as she smiled from ear to ear, and reached out to embrace her. It had been a few days since they had seen each other, and Jeannie was relieved to see a smile on Rose's face again. "I've missed you. You look good, sweetie. Did you sleep well?"

"As a matter of fact, I did." Rose knew they were all adults and decided she didn't have to hide anything.

"It was a most wonderful...*sleep*," she told Jeannie, as she smiled and looked out of the corner of her eye towards Frank.

"I'm so glad *it* was wonderful," Frank said.

"Well, now that we all realize how wonderful everything is, or was, or whatever, I need to talk to you two about an assignment. I know I told you not to come into work today, Rose, and it's fine for you to still stay home. I understand you're in good hands so I don't have to worry about you. I have some news. I wanted to pass it on to you both in person rather than waiting until you got to the office, or dragging you back to work when I had already threatened you to stay home one more day, Rose. The photo shoot in San Diego has been postponed, and I want to give you two the promotional project…the series of regional wedding shoots."

Rose was quite surprised. This must have been a quick change because the last boring staff meeting on Friday was all about San Diego.

"So why us on the promotional shoots, Jeannie? Those are always a big deal. You want us to do them?"

"Truthfully, we need two photographers who can make personal connections with these brides. We'd been waiting to announce who we would assign this project to, so we just tagged you both for the San Diego shoot until we made our final decision. I know you've been through so much lately, Rose. Are you sure you're up to this? If you're not, I'll understand."

"True, I have been through a lot. But I'm usually better if I throw myself into my work. You know that, Jeannie. I had been wanting this project, but I thought you had already given it to another team. At least that's what the rumor mill was saying."

"Well, you know if you ever want to know anything for certain then you need to ask me and no one else."

"But occasionally it's easy to believe what the masses gossip about."

"Well, now you know the truth. And here's the details. You'll be covering a total of six weddings over six weeks - one wedding each weekend. The days in between weddings will give you time to travel, come back home, and gear up for the next one. By the time the last wedding comes around, I have a feeling that one will yield your best work yet. Ideally, I want this project to not only be an award-winner for the magazine, but also something which gives six lucky brides a dream come true – having their wedding featured in a bridal magazine. It's good for dreams, and good for our magazine sales."

Rose and Frank smiled bashfully at each other, and at the idea of attending weddings together. But they tried to stay focused on Jeannie as she continued to speak. Rose was perfectly content sitting in a robe in her apartment talking business. It beat the hell out of sitting in a stuffy old conference room at work.

"The weddings will all be within a four to six hour driving distance so it won't be too much travel. And honestly, the road trips will be easier than flying with all your equipment, etc. Remember, you'll be shooting only six brides chosen from literally thousands of entries. This will be fast-paced, but also, a pleasant break from the norm."

"I really appreciate you trusting us with this one, Jeannie," Rose said appreciatively. "Is there anything else we can do for you?"

"I think that about covers it. I know you two have always worked so well together in the past, and this assignment will be very important to the magazine. I trust you two will still be able to work together now that you are doing other things together."

Rose leaned over to whisper in Jeannie's ear. "You caught me a little sooner than I expected. I would have dished about this when I saw you back at the office."

"Oh please, Rose. You're apparently the only one who didn't know this was inevitable. Everyone else already knew this man adored you."

Jeannie had spoken loudly enough that Frank heard every word, and Rose blushed until she could feel the heat radiating from her own face. Jeannie took one of Rose's hands, and Frank took the other.

"And while I appreciate your discretion, it's all over the office already. Don't be embarrassed. The whole place is thrilled."

Rose didn't think she could blush any more than she already had, and she began to feel as though this was some sort of out-of-body experience. She might as well accept it. It seemed as though everyone else already had. There was much rejoicing all around, so Rose rejoiced as well.

Frank walked over to the kitchen counter and poured Rose a cup of coffee. He added just the right amount of cream and sugar, brought it over to Rose, and sat it down on the table in front of her. Jeannie loved the way their working relationship had served as foreplay for their romantic relationship. They functioned as if they had been together for years.

"Thank you for the coffee, Frank. It's so good. Just the perfect amount of cream and sugar."

"No problem, dear."

It was as if he'd been training ever since he met Rose just to have the pleasure of bringing her a simple cup of coffee one morning. And it was obvious to Jeannie she didn't need to worry about these two.

"The first wedding will be in two weeks," Jeannie added. "I will be giving you an itinerary at the office tomorrow, and you will need to take some time to map out your ideas and plans ahead of time. Just as I mentioned, there will be a wedding every weekend. You'll have two weeks after the last wedding to turn in the final pictures, and then we'll all work on the magazine spread together."

Rose thought for a moment. Between losing Lily, being with Trevor, and coming home to a very loyal Frank, her life was all over the place. But she knew it was important to go the extra mile. "Sign me up, Jeannie," Rose said willingly and enthusiastically. "I've got this."

"And you, Frank?" Jeannie said.

"You heard the lady. We've got this."

"Alright. I'll speak to the publishers as soon as I get back. And I'll send out an email to the rest of the staff stating that I've assigned this project to you two. Take the rest of today to enjoy yourselves, and Rose, to gather your thoughts. I appreciate your willingness to come back to work so soon after your loss. I knew you were amazing, but you've just proven yourself all over to me with this comeback."

"Frank, hurt her and I'll fire you. And then I'll kill you. She's my girl. Take care of her."

"Yes ma'am. She's a strong and stubborn gal, but I'll do my damnedest to make sure she never gets hurt again."

"I'm holding you to that, Frank. I love this gal."

Jeannie seemed to believe they belonged together, and Rose hadn't had a chance, or the nerve, to tell her what had happened with Trevor. Now Rose wasn't even sure she could ever tell Jeannie all that had happened. And if she couldn't tell Jeannie, and she couldn't tell Frank, Rose felt as though she might burst. She needed to discuss Trevor with someone, but it seemed as though there was no right person to discuss him with. She missed Lily so much right now.

Jeannie told them both goodbye, and Frank walked out with Jeannie to her car. Rose closed the door behind them, still wearing her robe, and stayed inside to enjoy her coffee, courtesy of Frank. She anxiously waited for Frank to come back inside so they could talk.

"Rose, I really like this assignment. Promotional work for the magazine almost always goes to the old dogs who have been on staff forever or to someone who has been really kissing up. And now, we got it! How do you feel about it, Rose?"

"I'm excited about it as well. I honestly didn't think I would get this sort of project from the magazine for a few more years. I know it's because of you though, Frank."

"That's funny, Rose."

"Why is that? What's so funny? I mean it. You're older than I am, and I mean no offense. But you've been at the magazine longer, and in the business longer, and even you're excited. What makes you think I had anything to do with it? You have to know unless you were my partner, hell would have frozen over before I got a chance like this."

Frank walked over to her, put his hands on her shoulders and looked directly into her big green eyes.

"My dear, deals like this don't get dumped in my lap unless someone thinks I can handle it. You make me better than I am, Rose, personally and professionally. I think we could be a good *team*."

Rose knew he didn't just mean a photography team either. But she had to let it sink in a while longer.

"You don't have to think about the last part right now. But please think about it eventually," Frank added.

Rose certainly never thought of herself as being an asset to anyone. She wondered if Frank could really be right. She was moved by all which had been said during the last hour or so. So much to take in, and such a short amount of time in which to absorb it. And now, she contemplated the idea of being a team with Frank, in the office, in the bedroom, and in life.

"We are a good team, Frank. Personally and professionally."

"Rose, we're both somewhat responsible for where each other is right now, without even realizing it. You're strong in the places where I'm weak, and I'm experienced where you're still new. We complete each other. It's seldom a pair of photographers in this line of work find this sort of happy place where both parties benefit so completely from one another. In every way. How could I want any more?"

He walked over to hug her, because with Jeannie there, he hadn't had a chance to properly say good morning to her. Frank ended his little rant, took Rose in his arms and kissed her. He craved the feeling of his mouth next to hers, and he continued to kiss her as though it were as important as breathing. He needed her like he needed air.

"And this robe. Where did this robe come from? Because the last thing I remember you wearing was this."

And with that statement, he untied the loosely knotted belt around her waist and opened the robe to her naked body underneath. He looked at her like she was the Christmas present he'd always wanted.

"Now *this*, this looks much, much better."

He put his hands inside the robe and wrapped them around her soft, warm body. Frank loved the way she felt, and Rose gained a sense of peace and relaxation when he touched her. Though she would be lying if she didn't still remember the way Trevor's hands had felt on her body.

"Frank, do you think we could begin talking about those travel plans and strategies now?"

"It's good to see you so excited, Rose, but I had plans to be excited about something *else* before we got to work."

He began to kiss down her neck. She closed her eyes, and flashed back to the hotel, with Trevor, and all that happened there. The desk, the bed, everything. Rose had tried so desperately not to think of him, but it was difficult. Only one day of her life had passed since she had seen him, though she was certain it had been decades.

Rose knew she had to rescue herself from those thoughts. It was dangerous to be intimate with one man while thinking of another. She reminded herself over and over that Trevor was engaged, and that she probably wouldn't ever hear from him again. She knew they had come together at a time when they both needed something. It made sense to her as she attempted to rationalize the idea in her mind. But she would always remember that the last words she spoke to Trevor in person were, *I love you*. And a tear rolled down her cheek.

"Rose, you're crying. Why?"

Frank wiped her cheek with his hand. Rose never answered him. She couldn't. Frank had been so good to her, and she couldn't possibly tell him why she was really crying. But she felt horrible inside for letting him believe it was because of Lily.

Frank closed her robe and tied the belt back around her waist just as he had found it moments before. He loved her. The sex would always be there, but right now, he knew Rose needed human companionship much more.

"You know, dear, things have really moved fast the past few days. I think you've held up remarkably well. In fact, I don't even know if I could have kept moving at the pace you have."

Rose felt a sick feeling in her stomach again. One which reminded her losing Lily wasn't the only reason she was crying and in pain. She had confided in Frank before, but she couldn't possibly tell him of her experience with Trevor. Rose wiped the remaining tears from her own cheeks.

"I'll be better off if I could just go ahead and work. I know you think you're doing me a favor by keeping me from it, but it's my heart and soul. Could we just have some more coffee and sit together and work? And maybe later, after I feel I've gotten something accomplished, we can have *pizza*."

"I would never argue with a beautiful woman, Rose. Especially about *pizza*."

Rose embraced him, and clung to him. She needed to find a way to shake her memory of Trevor, once and for all. He would move on with his life, and she had a chance at being truly happy now with Frank. She didn't have to die inside because of what had happened with Trevor, which at one point, is what she felt might happen.. But Rose would make it all work, and Frank never needed to know about Trevor. It would only hurt him.

Frank realized how much Rose needed some food and a little more coffee. They talked excitedly about their plans for the new project while they put together a snack in the kitchen. Rose loved listening to Frank's logic and planning strategies, and he loved listening to Rose's emotionally fueled, youthful take on things. As they shared brunch, they each made notes on their cell phones and calendars, and Rose typed notes on her laptop.

She returned to work the next morning. Frank stopped by his house for some clean clothes since he only had one change at Rose's apartment. They hadn't discuss who would leave clothes and spare toothbrushes where. Things would simply progress on their own. They were so engulfed in their work and, in their feelings for one another, they allowed things to happen naturally.

The first week after they had received the promotional assignment, work went by so quickly. Rose found herself in a frenzy of ideas, notes, to-do lists, and alarms to remind herself of deadlines. It almost seemed like more than she could possibly get done. Sometimes she found herself spending the night at Frank's house, and sometimes he went home with her. They tried to still give each other personal space so not to wear out their welcome with one another too soon, but whatever they were doing was working for them.

Occasionally, Rose would still look at her cell phone, not to check her calendar or work notes, but secretly hoping there would be a message from Trevor. Just a *Hi* or *Hello* or *I miss you*. Something. Anything. Sure, it would hurt, and probably even make her cry, but at least it would let her know she hadn't given her love away in vain.

And yet, no message ever came. So there was still a part of her unable to move on. Once again, Rose tried to move forward. As painful as it was, she honestly had no regrets. She had undeniable chemistry with Trevor, but it wasn't meant to be anything more.

And so had come her last day in the office before they left for the first wedding assignment. They would travel on Thursday, visit the wedding site on Friday, and photograph the ceremony on Saturday.

"Rose..." someone said, politely knocking on Rose's open office door.

"Jeannie, hello!"

"My dear, how are you doing? You're positively radiant. Can I attribute that to the assignment, or to your photography partner?"

"Well, a little of both, to tell the truth. I don't know where the happiness of this project stops and the enjoyment of Frank begins. It all blends together, and I just know that I'm very, very happy."

"You do look incredibly fulfilled right now, Rose. And I'd like to have lunch with you today. I know it's hectic, but I just want to go over a few things before you leave town."

"Okay, do you want me to get Frank to join us?"

"This is a girls only lunch, dear. I've missed you. Frank has had you all to himself, and he will for a few more weeks. Today, I get you all to myself."

"Duly noted. It's just about lunch time right now, isn't it? What time would you like to leave?"

"Right now is fine with me, Rose. I thought we could just walk down the block and grab a little sandwich or salad and chat."

"Sounds great," Rose said happily. She honestly hadn't spent much time with Jeannie since Lily died. Of course that was coincidentally about the same time things got complicated with Frank, so she had been preoccupied in a few different ways. "Let me grab my purse."

Jeannie and Rose walked through the office toward the front door. On their way, they passed Frank.

"Don't be jealous, Frank, but I'm stealing your best gal for lunch. We need some girl time."

"Aw, I can't come?" Frank said, as Jeannie and Rose both shook their heads back and forth. "Well, you ladies have fun then. I'll see you when you get back. I have plenty of time coming up to spend with Rose, so I'll let you have her just this once." He leaned down to kiss Rose on the cheek as she left, and Jeannie smiled.

Rose was grateful for the lunch invitation. They chatted about work and the upcoming weddings as they walked down the block. They finally stopped at a little bistro which many of the local office workers frequented. They were seated, put their purses to the side, and began to get down to business. Well, that's what Rose thought would happen.

## CHAPTER ELEVEN

"Rose, how long have I known you now?"

Rose thought it seemed like a very strange question. Jeannie had hired her, and she knew exactly how long they had known one another.

"Well, just a little over three years, I think."

The waiter came by and they both ordered iced tea, along with a soup and salad, and then continued their chat.

"Yes, it has been that long. And we've been really close the whole time, haven't we?"

Rose was really suspicious by now.

"Well, um, you know we have. I've told you things my own family doesn't even know about me. You know things about me I don't even know about myself."

Jeannie leaned forward across the table, bracing her elbows on the edge and crossing her hands in an almost praying position.

"I love you like a daughter, Rose. You've been a wonderful friend to me. Which is why I have to ask you now…"

She paused for a moment. No more words came out of her mouth. Rose felt nervous around Jeannie for the first time since her job interview.

"What is it, Jeannie?"

Their food arrived at the table, and they thanked the waiter. Suddenly, Rose wasn't sure she was still hungry.

"What else happened the weekend you went home for Lily's funeral?"

"What do you mean, what else happened?"

"Rose…"

Rose took her fork and moved her salad around on her plate. She knew Jeannie had seen through her. It was pointless to think she could have kept it all from Jeannie anyhow.

"I went to high school with Trevor, but we really never talked back then. I saw him at the funeral home, and we decided to go have a beer to toast to Lily's memory. The next thing I knew…"

"And…"

"Well, we made love. Or had sex, or whatever it was. I don't know exactly what the first time counted as."

"First time? There's more? Do tell."

Rose finally smiled. Jeannie had noticed something different about Rose and apparently felt left out by not hearing about it. Jeannie was her friend, and she wanted to hear all the juicy details.

"Yeah, there's more. It's complicated though. He's engaged. He lives in a small town, and both of their families are well-known in the area. We made love as though we were made for each other, Jeannie. But I know it will never work."

Rose fought back the tears as she recounted the events of her weekend away. She did her best to eat a few bites, but the memory of it was fresh in her mind again now. And though she cared deeply for Frank, talking about Trevor still made her sad.

"Oh Rose, why in the world didn't you tell me? No wonder you've thrown yourself back into your work. So when did things start with Frank? I'm confused."

Rose explained how Frank had kissed her in the office the day she found out about Lily. Then how she slept with him later that night. Then about her affair with Trevor over the weekend. And then how she came back to Frank when it was all over. Rose felt a bit embarrassed as she told Jeannie the whole story.

"Honey, it's a wonder you've had any room in your head for work after what you've been through. I thought maybe this was all about losing Lily. You've had a lifetime of love in just a few days. So have you heard from this Trevor again?"

"No, and I don't even know what that means. I know he'll end up going through with his wedding. I just wish he could have made some other contact with me so I didn't think it was all some ridiculous mistake on my part."

"My dear. Let me tell you one thing. I wasn't always this age. I've had a few affairs in my past, and things like this aren't always so easy to explain. So, one more question."

"Sure, Jeannie."

"How much of this does Frank know?"

"Well…"

"None of it, huh?"

"Not a thing, Jeannie. Not one damn thing. And if I've cried over Trevor in front of him, he thinks the tears are about Lily. I wouldn't hurt him for anything. Honest. I love Frank. I made love with him the night before I left for Lily's funeral. But then there was this thing with Trevor. I just went from not having sex or even a date in months, to being in some sort of crazy love affair with two men in the span of one weekend. Please tell me this isn't one of those conversations where someone tells me they're disappointed in me now."

"Oh hell, Rose, you know me better than that," Jeannie said. "I suspected some drama to come out of your mouth today, but nothing like this. I feel bad you didn't come to me sooner because you must have been about to explode to tell someone."

"I have, but you seemed so happy for me and Frank, so I didn't think I should tell you."

"Rose, you know you can tell me anything. I wanted you to purge because I knew if you didn't, it would prevent you from doing your best work. That's it. If you had kept all this bottled up, your head would have been in a fog and your photography would have suffered. I gave you this assignment because I truly believe you're the best person for it. If your heart is somewhere else, then your head won't be screwed on straight."

"Wow, that's deep, Jeannie. And it makes perfect sense. I feel so much better for telling someone. I would have told something like this to Lily, but…"

"I know, dear. I know. How are you handling that, by the way?"

"It may sound crazy, but I still feel her. Like she's watching over me. Like she's my guardian angel. We had an unbreakable bond, but I feel like she's still near me. I swear, Jeannie, she's with me. Please don't fire me because you think I've gone over the deep end."

"Oh Rose, you're so funny. I would be a fool to fire you. And I thought you knew more about what a crazy old woman I was or you obviously wouldn't have just said that. Let me tell you something. When I said you can tell me anything, I really meant it. I don't think you're crazy or slutty. I just think you're a wonderfully talented friend who has been around the world and back emotionally in a very short period of time. I wanted to give you a chance to confess whatever was bothering you so you could move on. I know for a fact these things can hold you back professionally when you need to perform. They can eat you alive. That's why I'm here, Rose. I'm not just your boss, I'm your friend. And today, I'm your priest. Please don't ever hold things in. It's just not healthy."

Jeannie reached across the table and took hold of Rose's hand. Rose cried just a little, but she was getting used to controlling the tears. She'd been doing a lot of that lately. Rose thanked Jeannie, they finally ate lunch, and then walked back to the office together. Just before they entered the office, Rose hugged Jeannie again. No words were necessary.

They opened the office doors and walked back inside. As usual, the magazine staff was busy but enjoying themselves. Rose was so lucky to work in this office and so lucky to love her career. She almost skipped like a schoolgirl back to her office and began to gather her thoughts before the weekend trip.

"I trust you ladies enjoyed your lunch," Frank said, appearing in her office doorway.

"It was delightful. Mostly business stuff, you know."

Somehow, Frank didn't believe her, but it wasn't really important. Rose was smiling, and she seemed carefree, so he hoped whatever they talked about had been therapeutic for her.

The end of their work day came quickly. Frank and Rose left, waved goodbye to everyone in the office, and took off for the first wedding of their new assignment. Frank had traveled so much in his career, and had made packing a fine art and could complete it in an incredibly short amount of time. Rose, well, she was another story entirely. Rose packed for each shoot as though she might get stranded for months and need hundreds of changes of clothing for each of the four seasons. Frank thought it would be best if they just stayed at her place that night. Her preparations would surely take longer that his own, but maybe he could entice her not to take so long by suggesting *pizza*. He would stop by his place and pack, and then drive to her apartment for the night. They would leave from there the next morning.

And so Thursday morning came. The first location was about a four hour drive away, but they had to pick up a rental car and get all their luggage and camera equipment together. They would also need time to charge equipment once they arrived, unload their gear, eat, and get some rest. Rose had been far too excited to rest well. Knowing that, Frank made coffee and had it waiting when she woke up. But rather than dragging, she hopped right out of bed. She believed talking to Jeannie had been the best thing for her. Now, she was ready for a road trip.

As they drove, they talked, like always. They listened to music and even sang out loud. Neither of them had any talent for singing, but they were enjoyable moments nonetheless. They held hands and offered to drive when they saw the other grow weary. When they arrived at the hotel, they checked in, unpacked, and began to charge their equipment. It was always important to have the cameras and lights with a full charge at the beginning of a busy day, and tomorrow certainly would be just that. As exhilarated as they were, they were both a little tired, and wanted to save all their energy for the next day. Frank called room service and ordered a small pizza and salad to share, along with a couple of beers. Not wanting to end up with another incident of running to the door half-naked, they decided to wait until *after* room service arrived before making love.

The next morning, they awoke and laid in the comfort of each other's arms for a few minutes before beginning their busy day. It felt right somehow that particular morning to just hold one another tightly and save sex for later. Mentally, they had already begun a day of work, but they still took a few moments to kiss before they left the bed.

"Rose, sweetie, why don't you get in the shower first?"

"Are you saying I take longer than you, sir?"

"Well, no, not exactly, I'm just saying you might…well, yes, I guess that's what I'm saying."

"Very funny. But it's true. I do take longer. I'd love to get in first, if you don't mind."

"Not a problem at all, dear. It's just a pleasure to share the room with a beautiful woman such as yourself."

Rose smiled, kissed him with a little peck on the lips, and moved on with her toiletries toward the shower. Frank thought this would be a good time to unplug everything, wrap up the cords, and store them back in the equipment bags. It would be one less thing for Rose to worry about.

As he ritualistically packed his equipment, he noticed her rechargeable battery had not been plugged in completely overnight and may not have charged. He inserted it in her camera to check the charge level. The battery was most likely a spare, and it would probably be okay for a while, but still, he wanted to check it out for her. When he turned the camera on, he took a picture to test the battery strength, and then went back to view the picture. He accidentally flipped back twice rather than once, and there was a picture of a man, naked. Frank was surprised, and rightfully deciphered this was not a work-related photo. The majority of Rose's magazine photos involved women in bridal gowns, or at least men in tuxedos. Not naked men.

The date and time stamp on the picture were during the weekend of Lily's funeral. Suddenly, Rose's strange actions began to make sense. Frank knew he shouldn't, but he scanned through her other recent pictures and found even more. More of the same man lying on the bed, naked. More than enough evidence that there was physical intimacy involved. More than he wanted to see of a man who was obviously more than her friend. He didn't recognize the man, but he was well acquainted with the look on his face. It was the look of a man who had just had sex. And it was most likely with Rose.

He wasn't jealous, just shocked and confused. After all, he and Rose had made no formal commitments. He scanned through the remainder of pictures left on her memory card. Finally, after all the naked photos of this man, there were pictures of the same man standing in the hotel courtyard with clothes *on*. A refreshing change after all the naked photos, Frank thought. He wasn't upset with Rose, but he wondered what the story was, and why she was with this man at a time when Frank thought she was alone with no one to comfort her.

Frank heard the shower water stop and decided to put Rose's camera back as he had initially found it. The discovery of the low battery charge would have to be her own. And he would need to wait to see if Rose decided to talk to him about the subject of her photography. He wasn't angry, or sad or hurt. Just confused. And quite a bit curious.

He walked into the bathroom as Rose was stepping out of the shower and handed her a towel from the rack. It was freshly heated from the towel warmer, and she appreciated the service from her towel boy.

"Thank you, Frank. How thoughtful."

It was all Frank could do to keep his hands off her, especially dripping wet just out of the shower. He wanted her more than ever, despite the pictures he had seen. They didn't matter to him. Whatever happened had already happened. And he knew he had been with her almost every waking moment since Lily's funeral, so he didn't read too much into any of it. He would always want her. Always.

"Your turn in the shower, Frank."

"You're sweet, Rose."

Rose wanted to return the favor to Frank, so she made sure there was a towel on the warmer ready for him when he stepped out of the shower. She had grown to truly care for him and, since confessing all about Trevor to Jeannie, she felt much more at ease. And with no texts or contact from him whatsoever, it was becoming easier to forget him. Well, as easy as it would ever be.

Rose dressed, dried and styled her hair while Frank showered. While putting on her makeup, she noticed Frank had packed up all his chargers and cords. How efficient he was. She walked over to get her own equipment and noticed her battery charger had not been completely plugged in.

"Damn it," Rose said when she realized what happened.

Frank stepped out of the shower as he heard her. He already knew what was wrong, but he had to ask anyhow. "What's wrong, dear?"

"I apparently didn't have this camera battery charging properly," she said loudly so he could her hear from the bathroom. "Doesn't look like I had it plugged in well and it didn't charge completely. I still have an extra one, but I always hate it when this happens. Let me test it."

Frank knew what she was getting ready to do. She placed the battery inside the camera to test it, just as he had done. She suddenly remembered the photos of Trevor were still on her memory card. She quickly tried to look back through them, but only saw a few before the camera shut down. The battery was indeed dead. She froze for a moment, and began to recall those hours in bed with Trevor, and all the things they did together. She had tried so hard not to think of him. Rose worked quickly to get it all back out of her head before Frank saw them. But little did she know.

Just then, Frank walked out of the bathroom, completely naked, towel drying his hair.

"Thanks for the warm towel, doll. Don't worry about the camera battery. I know you have an extra. We'll plug it up right now and it will be fine."

Frank reached to take the camera and remove the battery for her, but she held it as though it were glued to her fingers.

"Thanks, sweetie, but it's my stupid mistake. I'll take care of it." Rose was so rattled, she looked as though she had never before operated a camera.

"Baby, don't let it get you all flustered." He knelt down beside her. He knew exactly why she was trembling, but it would ruin everything to tell her. "It's okay. Everything is okay. I promise."

Rose took her camera and sat on the corner of the king-sized bed she shared with Frank. Business partners and lovers. Sharing a bed on work time. These thoughts went through her mind while she struggled to move the pictures of Trevor from her memory card onto her laptop. Her mind was in overload. She needed the wedding rehearsal this afternoon to help take her mind off things. Working would be good. Yes, she needed to work.

Rose watched the photos appear on her computer screen, one by one. There was Trevor, looking at her high atop the hotel balcony with his mirrored sunglasses. Then there was Trevor on the bed. Rose had to bite the middle knuckle on her index finger to keep from saying anything as she looked at them. She thought she had pushed the memories of it all further back in her mind. Apparently she hadn't.

She loaded up her equipment along with the spare battery. Thank goodness for the spare battery. She couldn't afford any more mental field trips this weekend. It was essential she be focused and professional. Fortunately, she was there with a man who was both those things. She couldn't let what happened with the camera battery distract her for the rest of the day.

Rose and Frank walked out to the rental car and, after loading all the necessities, checked the itinerary for the rehearsal location. He programmed the address into the car's navigation system as she read it aloud to him, and they waited for directions. Frank had offered to drive. Rose, still a bit shaken from earlier and appreciative of his offer, agreed.

"You okay, sweetheart?" Frank asked.

Rose was nervous about the pictures, nervous about the assignment, and nervous around Frank, though she had no idea he knew why.

"I'll be fine…you know I just get jittery sometimes on these shoots. And…"

"Yes, dear? What is it?"

Rose looked up to the roof of the car and thought of sweet Lily, and wondered where she might be bouncing around in the afterlife. She hoped it was easier than Lily's earthly life had been. Lily deserved that much. She closed her eyes, crossed her fingers, and wished Lily would give her some idea of what to say or do right then.

"Oh, damn it, my nerves are just shot," Rose told Frank. "I forgot what I was about to say. But I'll think of it soon." She desperately tried to put it all behind her.

## CHAPTER TWELVE

Before Rose knew it, they were at the rehearsal, and the whirlwind of finding out about the assignment and all their planning was about to materialize before their eyes. They decided to carry their cameras with them, just to get a few shots that night. But most of the afternoon and evening would be all about getting to know the bride and groom and their families, seeing where everything would take place, and observing the lighting and location. This was actually the first wedding Rose had attended in quite a while.

Rose and Frank spent a few minutes getting to know the wedding party, the family, and studying the ceremony and reception areas. They made some preliminary pictures to get an idea of the lighting for the next night. They also made some notes to prepare their own thoughts for the couple's big day tomorrow. Rose had forgotten the thrill and emotion that went into wedding planning. From the time a girl can dream, she dreams of her wedding day. Well, most girls. Rose had never felt that way, but that's what she saw in this young bride's face.

The next night, Rose and Frank were astounded at how many places a photographer needed to be at one event at the same time. So much was taking place, and there were many wonderful opportunities. They worked hard, but still found time to party a little with the guests, as well as with the bride and groom. Everyone was excited for their presence there, and about appearing in the magazine. Rose and Frank practically felt like celebrities.

The morning after the wedding found them a tad weary, but exuberant nonetheless. They would travel back home for clean clothes and a brief break before heading back out on the road again.

That Sunday was a special day for Rose and Frank as they rested from one wedding and prepared for another. Rose felt this radically different assignment was a welcome distraction from Trevor. The road trips were a nice way to constantly be in new surroundings. If Rose was behind the wheel, she sometimes used the time to talk silently to Lily about all the things in her life that had happened since she died. If Frank drove, then Rose studied the itinerary for their next wedding. But she never wanted to look more than one wedding ahead on the list. Since Lily's death, Rose felt a strong sense to focus only on the present. It was clear to her now that no one was guaranteed anything beyond the present.

When Rose and Frank arrived back home from the first wedding, they both needed time in their own respective places to check mail, gather clean clothes and repack before heading out on the road again. By now they had alternated spending nights at each other's residences. The short time away in a shared hotel room had made them realize how much they craved one another's warmth in bed each night. When early Thursday morning came, Rose felt she had barely had enough time to unpack before she found herself packing the suitcase again and heading out to the next wedding. But sharing this hectic, yet exciting assignment, with Frank made it all the better. It was such an adventure.

Time seemed to fly by as the weeks passed, and Rose and Frank soon found themselves at the fourth wedding. They regretted that the assignment was already half over. It was the best time they had ever had on the job, and they had learned to read each other's minds so much that words weren't even necessary at times. As they laughed with the bride and groom and their families after the reception that night, the bride's father asked Frank and Rose how long they had been married.

"We're not married, sir," Frank said. "but I certainly do love her."

Rose was shocked and, yet, she wasn't. She knew he loved her, but he just hadn't said it aloud. And the first time he did was in front of virtual strangers with the remainder of a wedding cake just a few feet away from them.

"I would have bet money you two were married. I guess I should have looked for rings first, but I just assumed. You sure seem like you're meant for each other," the bride's father said, amazed that Frank and Rose weren't actually a married couple.

"I love him too, sir," Rose said to the man.

Frank looked back at her and smiled. He knew she loved him too, though maybe not exactly the same as he loved her. But he was a patient man, and he had waited so long to hear her say those words.

"Well, there you go," the father of the bride said to them both. "Why don't you two get some practice and feed each other a little of that leftover cake? There's plenty still, and all the guests are gone. Go ahead, I sure as heck paid for it. Someone should get some more use out of it."

And so, at the insistence of the bride's father, Frank and Rose decided to have a little fun. They slowly walked over to the leftover wedding cake. They gave each other silly looks as they cut two small pieces and fed them to one another, just like it was their own wedding. All the family left in the room applauded them. Rose finally felt she was moving on from Trevor. Maybe she would be feeding Frank wedding cake one day. At their wedding. Maybe.

Rose and Frank thanked the family for a wonderful evening, but the families were so honored to have them there and insisted the thanks went to them instead. With their cameras around their necks, the photographers walked out of the ballroom, hand in hand, with the taste of wedding cake still on their lips.

When they arrived back at their room, Rose knew it was time. She could wait no longer.

She took her camera from around her neck and carefully placed it on the hotel dresser. Frank began to remove the batteries for charging, as he always did when they returned from a wedding. But Rose asked him to stop.

"What is it, Rose?"

"I need to talk to you, Frank. Please. If I could just have a few minutes of your time."

"Of course, Rose. What is it?"

"There's something I need to talk to you about."

"Is it because of what I did earlier? When I told you I loved you for the first time in front of all those strangers?"

"No, Frank. I mean, I guess it caught me off guard somewhat, but I already knew you loved me. And you knew I loved you, too. It just came out like that, but I'm fine with how it happened. I have something else entirely to talk to you about."

Frank had a feeling it was related to the pictures he had seen on her camera a few weeks before. And he was right. Rose began to recall memories and details, much more than Frank wanted or needed to know, but Rose needed to purge. She told him everything. Every detail, every position, every kiss, every embrace. And when she was done, Frank wiped away the tears that had built up during her account of that weekend.

At least she had finally explained it, and of course Frank was sympathetic and forgiving. But he also had something to confess, and now was obviously the time.

When Rose had finished her confession, and all the tears which accompanied it, Frank began to speak. He told her how he, by chance, had found the pictures of Trevor on her memory card when testing her camera battery. He confessed to looking beyond the one photo he stumbled upon, and how he had remained curious but silent since he had found them. She was completely ashamed and attempted to explain herself, though Frank asked for no apology and no explanation.

"Rose, you're beautiful and wonderful, and I always assumed you had other love interests. I never once considered the fact I would win you easily."

"Frank, that's ridiculous. Lily is the one who always won hearts, not me. I stood in her shadow."

"My dear, for what it's worth, you're more than you know. In fact, you're the only one who doesn't realize your own value. Lily saw the value in you, it's you who never saw it in yourself. You simply never figured it out while she was still alive."

The lighthearted evening had grown deep with discussion. Much had been confessed and stated and admitted. They had both publicly said they loved each other for the first time in a room full of people.

And then they fed each other wedding cake. It had been quite an evening. Sleep seemed to solve so many problems in life, and so they concluded their discussion by falling asleep in one another's arms.

Each day afterward proved a forward progression in their relationship. Details had been revealed, questions had been answered, and their understanding of one another continued to grow with each day they spent together. That fourth week of the assignment had seemed to pass quickly and, far too soon, they found themselves at the fifth and next to last wedding.

Life seemed good, and for the first time in a long time, it even seemed simple. Rose had been the busiest in her career to date. She was enjoying the time with Frank, she was coping with the loss of her friend, and weeks had gone by since she had been in touch with Trevor. The distance from her everyday life, and from Trevor, had proved beneficial. Rose appreciated routine, but she truly needed this change. Watching so many happy couples at these weddings had almost restored her faith in life, and in love.

It wasn't until the end of the night after that fifth wedding when Rose got back to the hotel, took off her shoes and relaxed, that she realized the location of the next wedding. She stared at the itinerary over and over and over. It couldn't be…

Frank walked over to her and asked what was wrong. He took off his shoes. "I've never danced so much in my life. Not at a night club, not at a party. Nowhere in fact."

But Rose had a look on her face that told him he should change the subject from how his feet felt.

"Rose, it's late, dear, and we're both really tired. Don't worry about the itinerary right now."

"Frank, I think we might have a problem."

Frank removed his socks and shoes, sat them on the floor, and walked over to sit on the edge of the bed next to Rose. She handed him the itinerary. At first the location didn't mean anything, but then he noticed the names of the bride and groom and he understood her statement.

"Rose…"

"I know, but what the hell can we do? It's the very last wedding. It's not like I can back out. I never looked ahead at the itinerary because I only wanted to focus on one wedding at a time. I mean, I think I might have initially scanned over it, but I never saw this Frank, I swear."

And yet there it was as plain as day:

Trevor Barton and Stephanie Ryder

"How did I miss this, Frank? I would have told Jeannie before we ever left home if I had seen this. She already knew something was different with me. That's why she took me to lunch that last day I was at work. She knew I needed to get something off my chest before I left for this trip. She warned me that I couldn't be as creative and professional if I was dragging around emotional baggage, so I confessed it all to her. She was right. And now look, Frank. My baggage chased me down and found me. I'll be photographing their wedding."

Frank took her in his arms and kissed her tenderly. "My dear, we'll *both* be photographing their wedding."

"Frank, I love you. I really do. But right now I'm mad. I'm really, really angry. I worked damn hard to get Trevor out of my system. I put all my concentration on my job and on you, and now I have to see him again."

"Is that all it takes, Rose? Just seeing him? Is that enough to make you want him all over again?"

"I, I—I just meant that it all makes me mad. I cared for him the couple of days we were together, but it was intense, like a lifetime crammed inside a weekend. I didn't mean for any of it to happen, and when it was over, it was over. And I've done my best to get him completely out of my system, but I don't know what will happen when I see him again. I'm sorry to have to admit that to you. I never thought I would have to. I'm just so damn angry."

Frank grabbed her shoulders and kissed her hard this time. Harder than he ever had. Rose didn't know what to think. He had never kissed her that way before. She tried to pull away to ask him what he was doing, but he just pressed himself up next to her even harder. He put his whole mouth around her mouth and kissed her, rolling his tongue over her lips. He held her chin steady with one hand and used the other hand to reach around to the small of her back and hold her tightly to him. She struggled for a moment to free herself from his arms, not because he scared her, or because she didn't like it – because she did - but because she wanted to know why he was being so aggressive. Finally, Frank loosened his hold on her and let her speak.

"What was that, Frank?"

"You said you were angry. Well, it makes me angry, too. Damn it, Rose. I cared for you long before he did, and hell, I'll still care about you even if you go back to him. It pisses me off to see you like this. All during the wedding tonight, I had so much fun dancing with you. I waited all evening to be alone with you. Now this whole situation with Trevor comes up. It makes me mad, and I see that it even makes you mad, too. Just take it out on me, Rose. Take your anger out of me. Make love to me angrily. I don't care. Give it up for me like you would for Trevor."

Rose wanted to cry, but she was too mad. Frank was right. She really was angry. And she needed something to do with her anger. So, without a word, she began to jerk her clothing off as quickly as she could, never minding buttons or latches, just yanking it all off. It was all in the way. Yes, she was angry, but it was arousing to see Frank like this. It was a whole different side of him she had never seen.

As she shed her clothing, he quickly did the same. When they were both completely naked, Frank reached under Rose, picked her up, and carried her to the balcony of their hotel room. He kicked the chairs out of the way with one of his feet until there was enough space to lay Rose on the table in the moonlight. He left her spread out as if she were on display, and gave her a look that said *don't move a muscle*.

"Don't you dare close your eyes, Rose. I want you to know what a man who is really in love with you looks like while he's having sex with you. There's a difference, and I want you to see it for yourself. Otherwise, you'll never know."

Rose was still in shock, but it was one of the hottest moments she'd ever had. With any man, even Trevor. Frank kept looking at her, directly into her eyes. He leaned over her, placed one hand on her hips, and sank himself deep inside her. Rose threw her head back and closed her eyes in ecstasy. He leaned over her closer, placed both hands on both sides of her hips, and thrusted again and again.

"I told you not to close your eyes, Rose..."

She belonged completely to him right at that moment, and she would have done anything he asked. Anything. Rose loved knowing how angry Frank was. He was jealous of the idea that another man could take her away, and furious Rose might let it happen. Things had always been so sweet and loving with Frank. But there was a fire burning inside him ever since he had seen those pictures on her camera. He had been nice long enough. This was the woman Frank loved, and he needed her to know he had no intention of giving up on her.

The sex with Frank grew more intense with every move. She focused on his eyes, just as he had told her. Something was there. Not a sparkle or a twinkle. No words could explain it. Rose saw trust and concern and seasons shared and years ahead together. She saw everything she knew Frank had saved up to give her one day, if only she allowed him to do so. She focused on those eyes of his, so blue, and so true to her. But she also focused on the incredible pleasure from him, each time he moved in and out of her, until finally he yelled out as he finished. Not once had he unlocked his eyes from Rose's stare. Never mind the noise they made, or that they were on the hotel balcony, though it was mostly obscured from view. As far as they knew, the moon and stars had been their only witnesses. Frank looked at her, still breathing heavily, and took her hands inside his. He pulled her to sit upright again and then kissed her. Much slower, and less aggressively, and then he embraced her sweetly. They clung to each other as their breathing returned to normal.

"Rose, did you see my eyes? Do you know why I made you stare into my eyes?"

Rose, still surprised from the very different kind of sex with Frank, did not answer, but merely shook her head back and forth.

"I wouldn't let you take your eyes off me for a reason, Rose. I love you. And even though that was intense, I know my eyes conveyed something no words that I ever say to you could. And I know when we arrive on site to photograph their rehearsal, you'll see Trevor and you won't be able to help yourself. There's a part of you that thinks you still want him. So I want you to go to him, Rose. Go to him. It wasn't anything you thought you wanted until you were with him. Go and be with him one more time to see if it's something you still want. I'll be fine. I'd rather you know for sure. And if it takes you being with him once more to figure it out, it's a small price to pay. At least I won't have to spend the rest of my life wondering about it. But now, now you know what it looks like when someone is in love with you while making love with you. So you look in his eyes when you're with him, Rose. If you see the same thing you saw in my eyes, then maybe you really do have a difficult decision to make. But I honestly don't think that will be the case."

As painful as that was for Frank to say, and for Rose to hear, it made them feel closer somehow. He helped her down from the table and back inside the hotel room, and they cleaned up and crawled into bed together. Rose was apprehensive to cuddle with Frank, not knowing if he was upset about her feelings for Trevor, but she moved over next to him anyhow. He did want her there, and he held her so tightly, with one arm beneath her and one arm across the top of her.

"I didn't hurt you in any way, did I, Rose? I would never, ever want to hurt you. But I suppose I've been more tense about it than I thought. I just knew I had to do something drastic to prove the way I feel about you. I've been with a lot of women, and I know the difference between a look that says *I'm really enjoying this sex* and *I really care about you*. It's easy to get love and sex mixed up, especially when one or both parties are hurting. Like when Lily died. I'm not condemning you for having a fabulous physical weekend with Trevor. I have absolutely no right. I'm just asking you to see the difference. You saw my eyes, Rose. I let you see everything about me while we were out on that balcony. I let you look deep into my eyes and all the way into my soul. If you can do that same thing with Trevor, then I'll understand, but I wanted you to see it in me first."

"You didn't do anything to hurt me, Frank. It was actually really hot. I've never felt more wanted by you. Besides, I know you would never hurt me. I knew exactly what you were doing, and I trusted you every second. I trust you with my whole body and soul. But I do feel strange about you offering me permission to figure out things with Trevor one last time."

"Don't feel strange about it, Rose. It's not that it won't mean *anything*. It's just that I don't think he loves you the way I do. Still, I know there's a question in your mind. If I thought he was making love to you like I just made love to you, well, I wouldn't like that at all. But I want you to see it, Rose. You have to see it for yourself. You need to see it for yourself."

Rose wanted to argue with him, but she knew it was futile. She did still need to know for certain. And it almost made her love Frank even more for offering her the opportunity to find out, on her own. However she had to do it.

They slept like babies the rest of the night, exhausted from their buildup and release of sexual tension. When they awoke the next day, they headed to the sixth and final assignment destination - Trevor and Stephanie's wedding.

## CHAPTER THIRTEEN

After weeks of absolutely no communication from Trevor, Rose awoke on Thursday to a text.

*"Rose...sorry I haven't texted lately. My dad's health worsened after Lily's funeral and he died two weeks ago. I wanted as much time with him as possible, so I only focused on him. That's why I haven't contacted you. Things have just been a mess. I get married this weekend and we couldn't change the date because there's supposed to be these people making pictures or something. I don't know much about it. It's mostly Stephanie's thing. Please let me hear from you one more time before I go through with this."*

All this time Rose had been angry with him for not contacting her, and his father had been sick and died. Rose had mistaken Trevor's lack of communication for a lack of concern. What if he really meant to try for more with her? What if he really *didn't* want to go through with his wedding? And it was obvious Trevor didn't realize she would be one of the photographers. Then she remembered Frank's offer.

But could she really accept his offer to be with Trevor once again? Rose still felt strange about it. She knew Frank loved her, but this text from Trevor changed things. She reluctantly showed Frank the text.

"Rose, I'm sorry. I know it's already going to be difficult enough for you to show up to his wedding, and I'm sure you feel guilty for this somehow now. Not that it's your fault in any way, but I know how you are. This doesn't change anything for me, though. I still love you madly, and you are still free to see Trevor in order to clear your head. I'm sorry for his loss, and I know you are as well."

Rose sat there after talking to Frank, reading the message from Trevor over and over. It was so hard to believe, but Rose needed to keep moving. Frank kissed her on the head to remind her of his constant love and friendship. Still, her heart was in turmoil.

The time came for them to pack up the car for the last wedding in the series of their special assignment together. This one was a little less exciting for them though, for obvious reasons. Frank was honestly being as kind to her as he had ever been. In fact, he was more in love with her now than ever. They tried to keep words short that morning as they prepared for travel and reserved conversation mostly for business until they arrived at their destination. They were fortuitously headed towards the same hotel Rose had stayed at when she came to town for Lily's funeral. The same hotel where the infamous weekend with Trevor had taken place. Now, she was on her way there with Frank to see Trevor marry another woman.

They began to cross the lake where Lily had met her untimely death. As Frank drove, which he had insisted doing on this trip, he looked at Rose's face. She looked like a little girl turning away from the scary part of a horror movie. She squinted her eyes and bit her lip to keep from crying. Frank reached over and took her hand, even though things were quite awkward between them.

"Anything I can do, love?"

Rose struggled to fight back the tears. This was much harder than she thought. But still, she moved forward because remaining professional was so important to her.

"I'll be fine, but can I just tell you one thing?"

"Anything, dear. What is it?"

Rose felt as though she didn't deserve Frank. He did everything for her without asking for anything in return. He was truly a beautiful man.

"Please don't ever forget how much I love you. Okay?"

"This trip won't be easy for either one of us, Rose. We both know it. But we'll be okay. I feel it."

And so they arrived at the hotel. That hotel. They parked the rental car out front and walked inside. Only a short time had passed since she had been there. It looked the same, but it felt different. Rose wandered off and began to stare aimlessly at pictures on the wall or the displays of events at the hotel. Frank went to the desk to take care of the room reservation. He could tell each time Rose reached out to touch something that it was for a reason. Rose seldom did anything randomly. There was much rhyme and reason to practically every move she made. If he wanted to love her, and he did, it was something he would have to accept. She finally walked over to sit on a sofa in the lobby, and Frank walked over to her after he had completed the registration.

He stopped by the sofa and bent down to embrace her. It was such a sweet embrace, and after they held their cheeks close together for a few moments, she stood back up and began to walk with him. They had much to gather from the car, and much to think about.

They made their way back to the parking area and gathered their things. Rose felt every familiar step there with Trevor. In around forty-eight hours, her life would be simplified in one way or another. She would either watch Trevor marry Stephanie, or he would change his mind to be with her. It felt so twisted and wrong somehow. Rose felt badly for even allowing her mind to consider an outcome where Trevor didn't get married by the end of the weekend. But her heart certainly entertained the notion.

Frank helped her with the elevator buttons as she simultaneously kept a tight grip on her camera equipment and luggage. He looked around at the hotel's décor and design features, and commented on how well-appointed it was. Frank had excellent taste. He wasn't pretentious, but he appreciated nice things. He was always someone she could be proud to be near. Frank was seeing it all for the first time, and oddly enough, so was Rose. There were so many things she had missed as a guest there last time. Aesthetically, anyhow.

They walked off the elevator and down the long and winding hall. It was frustrating to her, the way everything reminded her of the time with Trevor there. And now she was there with another man. Rose's mind wandered as she walked, and suddenly, that long and winding hall was already behind her. As Frank took out his card key to open the door to their room, Rose felt her cell phone buzz in her pocket. It would have to wait, since her hands were full, but she already knew who the message was from.

Frank heard it too, and he knew what Rose would do next. He knew what she had to do. After she sat down her luggage and equipment, she took out her cell phone. Frank continued to unpack his clothes and equipment, and, in a gentlemanly fashion, tried to give Rose privacy.

Rose read Trevor's text.

*"It's you, isn't it? You're the photographer for the wedding from that magazine, aren't you?"*

Well, at least he had figured that much out on his own. But so many difficult things were left to do over the next two days, regardless of the outcome. *At worst*, she would say goodbye to Trevor and photograph his wedding to another woman. She wasn't quite sure what the *at best* would be, or even if there was one.

Rose texted him back while Frank watched from their balcony. He gave her privacy she didn't deserve for a situation he didn't deserve to be mixed up in. Rose didn't like how this madness affected so many people at once, and it couldn't continue. She loved them both, but her anxiety level was climbing. This had to end.

*"Yes, Trevor. It's me. I only realized it was your wedding a few days ago, and then it was too late to change my assignment. That was probably around the time your dad died, which I'm so sorry for. I really feel horrible for you."*

Only seconds went by before Trevor returned her text.

*"I have to see you. Please don't say no. I know I'm getting married, or I'm supposed to be, but please."*

How could Rose possibly respond? Trevor just indicated his wedding might or might not take place. Though Frank offered for her to see him, she wasn't sure she could go through with it.

*"Are you sure that's a good idea, Trevor?"*

Then she saw Trevor's name and phone number appear on the screen of her cell phone, and she stared at it blankly, as though entranced. Rose made no movement whatsoever during the first ring.

A second ring also came and went.

## Rose, On Her Own

She played out a thousand scenarios in her mind of what would happen if she answered her phone, and they all scared her. She would answer and be weak at the sound of his voice. She hated that part about him. She had already told him goodbye. They had already shared a last embrace and had their last kiss. Rose couldn't possibly go back now.

A third ring.

Rose thought of those sweet little kisses he gave her when they parted. She suspected they were well-played and contrived, but she loved his farewell kisses so. The way he left his lips pressed firmly together for what seemed like minutes, but were only seconds. They were the kind of kisses that wouldn't lead to anything. They were full of will power not to allow anything else to happen, but they still felt lovely. She adored them. If she answered the phone, she would only find herself in the middle of one of the kisses again, most likely at the end of more lovemaking. And she wasn't sure she could suffer through another goodbye.

A fourth ring.

She had fought a valiant fight up until now, but she could hold back no longer. Rose didn't like that she wanted him, but she needed to know once and for all if he was truly who she wanted.

Despite her attempts to walk away from the phone, she surrendered. She hated herself for it, and knew she would feel weak at the sound of his voice.

"Rose, is that you?"

"Yes, Trevor."

"Where are you right now, Rose?"

"I just got to town. I'm at the hotel with my photography partner from the magazine and we're in our room."

"Which hotel are you at, Rose? Is it *our* hotel? Is it? That's where the wedding is supposed to be, Rose. But I guess you knew that already, didn't you?"

"Yes, Trevor. I'm at the hotel. Our hotel, your wedding location, whatever. I'm here. Well, *we're* here actually."

"I need to see you, just for a few minutes, Rose. Do you have a room of your own, or are you sharing a room with the other person from your magazine?"

"I'm sharing a room. Why do you ask?"

"May I stop by for just a minute? Please? I have to drop off something to the hotel staff for the wedding anyway. I can't stay, honestly. But I have to see you."

"Well, okay. I guess. We're in room 1689. You know how to find it."

They said goodbye and ended the call. Frank was still outside enjoying the view of the courtyard and the lake beyond, or at least pretending to.

She walked to the balcony door and looked at Frank. He was handsome and sophisticated. She stared at him once more, just in case her fortuitous meeting with Trevor was about to upset the fragile balance in her ever-changing universe. Frank honestly deserved better than what she was putting him through. He turned around and saw her staring at him. Whether she realized it or not, she was smiling at him. That moment changed everything for Frank.

He reached to open the door and Rose stepped out onto the balcony with him. He put his arm around her, and they stood looking out towards the lake together.

"So, this is where you grew up, sweetie?"

"Well, all around here, actually," she told Frank, waving her hand across the air to cover the land they could see in their view. "This hotel was built since I moved away from here, but if you look just over to the right you can see my high school and the pizza place where I used to work."

"So, you've always liked *pizza*, huh?"

It made them both laugh.

"That was Trevor on the phone, wasn't it?"

Rose didn't answer aloud, but just shook her head up and down.

"It's okay, Rose. I knew this was coming. I'll leave for a while so you two can talk."

"Frank, it's okay, you don't have to leave."

Just then, there was a knock, and Frank walked over to open the door.

"Yes?" Frank asked, looking at the man in the doorway.

"I'm sorry. I was looking for Rose Millican. I must have the wrong room," Trevor said.

"No, she's here," Frank said as he opened the door wider, not realizing who Trevor was.

"Trevor," Rose said, as she walked to the door. She took him by the hand and lead him into the room. "This is my photography partner from the magazine, Frank Harrington. Frank, this is my friend from high school, Trevor Barton."

It was awkward. Frank knew about Trevor, although Trevor had no idea about Frank. And Trevor had simply assumed any partner from work whom Rose shared a room with would have been female.

The men gave each other the public and obligatory handshake men give, whether they know or even like one another. Rose wasn't certain what to do next, but as always, Frank made it easy for her.

"I have some questions for the hotel staff regarding the ceremony and reception. I'm not sure where we're supposed to have some of the equipment set up," Frank said.

Rose knew it was an excuse, and though Trevor had only known Frank a total of about two minutes, he knew the same. This man obviously knew something which made him offer to leave the room.

Frank touched Rose's arm ever so slightly, but in a way only people who had been intimate would touch. "Do you need me to bring you anything from downstairs? A sandwich or snack? We haven't had a chance to eat since we arrived. I just thought you might be hungry."

"Well, maybe a soda or some sparkling water. Just something to settle my stomach a little."

"Sure, Rose," Frank said as he walked toward the door. "It was nice to meet you, Trevor. See you tomorrow at the rehearsal."

"Yeah, man. Nice to meet you, too. And yeah, see you tomorrow."

As Frank walked out of the room, Rose felt this was one of the oddest days of her entire life, and she only had seconds in which to process it. She didn't know how long Frank would be gone because there were no real questions to ask the hotel staff. But it looked professional enough to Trevor. And so now she was alone with him again, for the first time in a while.

"Rose, I guess I just assumed the other person from the magazine would be female."

"Well, Frank has been my photography partner for around three years now, and I've learned a great deal from him."

"You guys look close."

Intentionally changing the subject, Rose asked, "You wanted to see me?"

Trevor leaned in to kiss her, but she didn't fall into it immediately. When she finally succumbed, she cut it rather short and embraced him, resting her head on his shoulder.

"You're getting married in two days, Trevor," she said as held him close. She could feel his heart racing.

"Rose, I can't stay long." He pulled her away from his chest to look into her eyes. "The whole family is waiting on me at my house. I don't know what to do. I'm not sure I can go through with this. I've wanted to talk to you for weeks, ever since you left actually. But with dad being ill and the wedding plans snowballing by the day, I just haven't known what to do."

He leaned in to kiss her once again. She fought it with everything she had, but this was exactly what she had been afraid of. The kiss from Trevor melted her very soul, as well as every muscle in her body. She wasn't even sure if her legs would still work once she tried to walk again.

"Damn it, Rose, I need to go," he said, finding it difficult to leave her now that he had finally seen her again. "I swore to everyone I would only be gone a few minutes. And you already have me excited," he said, looking down towards the zipper of his pants. It was no secret he still wanted her. Rose pressed her lips together and tried not to smile as she looked down in that general direction. "It's not funny, love," Trevor said, though he grinned a little himself.

He certainly didn't look or sound like a man getting married to someone else in forty-eight hours.

"But seriously, I have to leave now. I want to see you sometime Saturday morning. I wanted to see you tomorrow, but with so much family here at the hotel watching me, there's just no way. They'll all be too busy to have their eyes on me the day of the wedding though."

"Trevor, how exactly do you mean, *see me*?"

"I think you know the answer to that question, Rose."

"Trevor, really? I mean, you're getting married."

"Like I said, it's all been snowballing. I didn't mean for things to ever really get this far, you know? I mean, I love her. But I'm not in love with her. I just don't think I can back out now, Rose. But I still love you. Can't we just keep seeing each other anyway?"

"Well, actually, Trevor, I don't think we can."

"Okay, I know that really isn't fair to you. I'm sorry. I just don't know what else to do. I have to go, and your friend Frank will be back soon. Let me see you Saturday before the wedding. Please. Just for a few minutes at least. Please, Rose."

"Text me later. But for now, you need to go."

As he left the room and shut the door behind him, Rose felt that chill again. The same chill she felt when he left her in the hotel room alone on the morning of Lily's funeral, after they had first made love. The same chill she felt when she thought she might never see him again afterwards.

Rose tried to collect her thoughts as she waited on Frank to get back from whatever pointless errands he had offered to run. She walked back out onto the balcony and noticed an afternoon rain approaching. No, please. Not rain. Not again. She continued to remember the soft, sad rain at the hotel that day after Trevor left, and the sad, sad rain at Lily's funeral later that day. Please, no more rain. If the sky began to cry, she knew she would, too.

She took a few deep breaths in an attempt to calm herself, but it hurt to even breathe. She wasn't sure if she was breathing *in* pain or breathing *out* frustration. Maybe both. Getting through these next two days would be a culmination of her personal and professional life. But she wasn't quite sure how to make things fall into place.

## CHAPTER FOURTEEN

While staring at the view of her hometown, and all that was different and all that was still very much the same, she felt a hand touch her shoulder. Then she felt another hand, pulling her hair away from her neck. She felt soft lips on her soft skin. Frank had somehow made his way back into the room without her noticing, but admittedly, she *had* been out of sorts for a few minutes.

"How did things go?"

"Well, it wasn't quite as perfect as I had imagined it, Frank. He's in a very strange place with losing his father so recently and not being able to postpone the wedding. It's all awkward for him. He's still grieving. And the presumed happiness one equates with premarital bliss is just something I've never really seen in him anyhow. Now add seeing me into the mix, and it's all even more awkward. He's really a nice guy, Frank. Honest. I wish you could have met him under different circumstances."

"He did seem like a nice guy, Rose."

"Frank, it's okay. I don't expect you to say anything in his favor after only a few seconds of brief acquaintance."

"Well, I'll never be able to know him under different circumstances, Rose. It's senseless to even think that way. I only know him now because of you. And, of course, knowing how you feel about him affects how I think about him. But I do know this. No matter what happens, he will always be someone you cared about, at least at one point in your life. All the things we've done in our lives have brought us to where we are now. I wouldn't be who I am without the things I've done or the people I've been with. And the same goes for you. Each person and event in our lives played a part in getting us to this day. I like who you are now, and you like who I am now. So it's hard to say we'd go back and change anything, you know?"

Rose thought it all sounded so eloquent when Frank said it.

"Sorry, Frank. I just think he's a really sweet guy who has been through some unfortunate things. We mourned Lily, and we share a common background. I'm really sorry all this happened."

"That's what I was just trying to tell you, sweetie. Don't live life with regret. You were with him, and you enjoyed it. Right?"

Rose thought she had never been asked such a bold question. How would she admit to one man how much she had enjoyed being with another man? But Frank had more than earned her honesty. So she thought honesty was the only option here.

"It was only two days, Frank. And I thought I was more of a grown woman, but it all truthfully made me feel like a silly little school girl again. I have no idea what came over me. In a way, it felt like those days with him lasted a lifetime when, in all actuality, they were almost over before they even started. But honestly, I'm really not sorry it all happened. I *don't* regret it. It felt fabulous and heightened all my senses. And it hurts me to say that to you because I care for you so much, Frank. I have no clue what to do right now. I'm caught between where I've been and where I need to be. I don't know how to get where I need to be. Help me, Frank. How the hell do I get to where I need to be?"

Frank sighed for a moment after Rose stopped talking, and then brushed her hair away from her face and kissed her. One soft, slow kiss.

"I'll help you anyway I can, sweetheart," he said after the kiss, "but you have to lead the way."

"Yeah, I was afraid you'd say that. He asked to see me for a while on Saturday."

"On the day of his wedding? Really? The idea that he wants to meet with another woman on the day of his wedding isn't necessarily what bothers me. What bothers me is that it's with someone I care about, and that someone is also my business partner. And photographing his wedding is our job right now, Rose. I want you to find your answers, I really do. But promise you'll still be able to work the assignment when the time comes. We *are* here on business."

"You're right, Frank, and I've always looked to you for my definition of professionalism since they paired us together at the magazine. You've been the best photographer I've ever known, and a wonderful friend. Not to mention an excellent lover. I promise no matter what answer I come up with, I'll be on time for everything on our schedule. You have my word as a fellow photographer, a friend, and someone who loves you very much."

"How about you and I go downstairs and get something to eat, and then get a good night's sleep tonight, my sweet Rose? I have a feeling we might just need the extra rest."

After a short but lovely meal at one of the hotel restaurants, they began to make their way back to the room. Rose passed by one of the ballrooms and realized it was where the wedding reception would take place. "Frank, do you know where the ceremony is being held?"

"Well, I've tried to be ready by knowing every little detail ahead of time." He reached down for her hand, and walked with her outside. She immediately heard the pleasant sound of rushing water. "The vows will be exchanged at the foot of this waterfall."

Frank walked her down the stairs to the bottom of the cascading falls. The water gently sprayed her face and the landscape lights made it possible for her to even see little droplets of water flying through the air. Except for the fact that this was where another woman would marry a man she still thought about making love to, it was a very nice place.

"I've never really asked you Rose, but do you know Stephanie?"

"No. You might have assumed I knew her from school, but I don't. Her family apparently moved into the neighborhood where Trevor grew up, but it was after I left for college. Plus, she's two or three years younger than me. In all the time we've talked, Trevor never said much about her. He hasn't even shown me a picture of her, and I haven't tried to find one. I mean, I didn't intend to sound asinine."

"I know, dear. I'm sure it's awkward at best. All of this. Sincerely, I know this is will be difficult. And I hope you let me do whatever I can to make this all easier for you."

"You might be sorry you said that, Frank."

Frank stopped, and although Rose was sure he was about to kiss her, all he did was embrace her, in a protective sort of way. He kept her close to his body, and the warmth felt nice next to her exposed shoulders on the breezy summer evening. He rested his chin on top of her head.

"My dear, I'm sorry for many, many things in my life, but being here for you right now, even in the midst of all this drama, is not anything for which I'm sorry. These past few weeks have been wonderful. Trying at times, dealing with so many emotional brides and crazy mothers of the brides and pissy bridesmaids. And even pissy groomsmen."

They both laughed. And when he saw that she had finally relaxed, he looked into her eyes, and *then* he kissed her. At the exact spot where Trevor would marry Stephanie. Frank knew there was little he could really do to alleviate any pain she would feel as the next two days unfolded, but right now, he could kiss her. Right there in the spot where Trevor would kiss Stephanie. But first, he wanted it to be the spot where Frank kissed Rose.

Rose knew Frank was a smart man in his career, and now she understood he was even more intelligent in the ways of love. He was so mature and patient, neither of which she felt described herself at this particular point in life. But this magnificent man held her dainty hand inside his and walked her back to their room.

Rose had been a little chilly on the walk, and Frank welcomed her into bed next to him. He made a silly face, and then pulled the down comforter over the two of them, like a child's blanket fort. They kissed until they fell asleep, in the safety, and luxury, of one another's warmth.

Neither Frank nor Rose had set an alarm for the next morning. Always for the day of the wedding, but never on the day of the rehearsal. It was their time, and they moved a little slower. The more leisurely awakening allowed their creative minds the opportunity to not only rest, but to explore and absorb all the sights and sounds around them. Their moods and approaches to life greatly influenced their work.

The first to wake up on the rehearsal day was Rose. She sat up, stretched her arms a little, and then pulled the cover back up to her chin. The movement she made was just enough to rouse Frank, and she apologized for waking him.

"Well, maybe you can do something to show me how sorry you are," Frank said to her with a grin.

"How about this then?" Rose leaned over to kiss him on each cheek, each eyelid, and each ear.

"That feels really nice, but I think you're running out of things I have two of." Frank looked at her with eyes that said *hint, hint*.

"Well, let me see what else I can find." She kissed his forehead, his chin, and then his chest. "Well, you *do* have two nipples," she said as she kissed each one, and then continued to slowly kiss all the way down to his belly button. "But I just can't seem to find anything else you have two of."

"I think if you keep looking, you might find something else I have two of," he said, eyes closed, and head tilted back just slightly.

As Rose continued kissing his body, she smiled. She knew how much pleasure she could give Frank. He always made her feel so special and precious. And Rose loved seeing how happy she made him. She teased him a bit more, and then kissed, licked, nibbled and sucked until he was completely satisfied. So satisfied that even though he had just awakened, he already wanted to sleep again. He held her under the covers again for a few minutes afterwards.

"That, my dear, was simply amazing. I'm not even kidding."

Rose just smiled and rolled her eyes around a little. "Aw, shucks."

"I mean, seriously. This hotel is filled with comment cards. I should fill out one and tell you how well *you* did."

"You're funny, you silly man. But you're worth every second of what I just did. No one has ever cared for me like you. And I didn't do that for you because I felt I had to. I did it because I wanted to. Because I adore my time with you. I love what a gentleman you are. I love how intelligent you are, how sexy you are, and I love how much you love me. And how much you warm me up when I'm cold," Rose said, still snuggling up next to him.

Suddenly, she threw the cover back and jumped out of bed. "I'm hungry, Frank. We have a long day ahead. How about we get some breakfast?"

"You mean, after the way you devoured me, you're *still* hungry?"

"Well, just a little."

Then Frank heard her stomach growl. Twice. "Okay, okay, I'm getting ready to go to breakfast with you, dear."

As they entered the restaurant area, they saw a large crowd entering the hotel, with loads of luggage and suit and dress bags in tow. Rose knew this must be the wedding party. There would be much for them to do that day. A few of them had young children. Rose didn't really envy them. At all. Dragging the kids and clothes and luggage around looked like an awful lot of work. She could barely keep up with herself some days.

Her eyes scanned the mass of people, but she didn't see Trevor. But that wasn't a huge concern to her right then. It was the rehearsal day, and she always saw both the bride and groom on rehearsal day. If she didn't see him now, she was certain to see him later. Rose realized if she continued to stare, she might finally see the bride. And she definitely wanted to wait for that, at least until after she had her morning coffee.

Yes, coffee. That's what Rose needed right now. As soon as they were seated at a table, she took the upside down cup in front of her and turned it right side up. When the waitress approached their table with a pot of fresh coffee and a smile, Rose was definitely appreciative. Frank immediately passed her the cream and sugar. Rose never tired of seeing his attentiveness to her every need, or his indulgence to most of her whims as well. As she added her own perfect blend of cream and sugar to her morning elixir, Rose thought of how Frank often did the sort of things a girl could really get used to. She felt like she could totally commit to him if it weren't for this mess with Trevor looming over her. She slowly sipped the hot coffee and began to mentally focus on the day's activities, while diligently trying to distance herself from its participants.

After a satisfying breakfast, much discussion, and, of course, coffee, they exited the restaurant and headed back to their room. There were itineraries to review and strategies to discuss. One can never be too prepared, Rose always told herself. And that was applicable to this weekend more than any other time in her life.

After they retrieved their cameras from the room and returned downstairs, Rose noticed a woman walking across the lobby. There wasn't anything striking about her. Her hair was ordinary, her clothes dull and matronly, and her makeup minimal. She looked rather lost, and stopped and stared aimlessly around her. Rose thought it seemed foolish that anyone be lost in this hotel, given all the staff available at any and every point of reference. Rose continued walking, and somehow she made eye contact with this woman. Perhaps this was someone she had gone to school with years ago, or someone from her old neighborhood. Rose thought how strange it was, how details of your past fade after they're not a part of your everyday life for a while. But this woman continued to follow Rose with her eyes. Rose thought it strange, and quickly tried to make a visual association with who the woman might be, but to no avail.

Rose whispered to Frank how strange it seemed that she couldn't place the face no matter how much she tried. "Don't worry about it, love. You're practically a celebrity here now. Besides, you're a great looking gal. Maybe the women think so, too," Frank said with a naughty grin and a little jab to Rose's arm.

"Oh, hush," Rose told him. "I'm serious. She just kept staring at me. Like she knew me. I've been stared at before, but this was different. I'm a little disturbed by it, Frank."

As Frank and Rose continued to walk through the high-ceilinged sunlit area of the lobby and down towards the conference rooms and ballroom areas, Rose felt a tap on her shoulder. "Excuse me," she heard a voice say to her.

"Are you by any chance here to photograph the wedding? The wedding here tomorrow evening?"

"Well, yes," Rose said, looking up at Frank. "Yes, we both are. Are you with the wedding party?"

"I suppose you could say that," the woman answered. "I'm the bride."

## CHAPTER FIFTEEN

The first time she met Stephanie was absolutely not supposed to happen this way. Rose had needed time to prepare. Time to make sure she had on a pretty outfit, or makeup. Or at least time to brace herself for meeting the woman who would marry Trevor. But, fate had placed them together. Here. And now.

"Then I guess that makes you Stephanie Ryder," Rose said, extending her hand as she nervously introduced herself on such short notice. "I'm Rose Millican, and this is my partner from *The Bride's Side* magazine, Frank Harrington."

Frank reached out to shake Stephanie's hand. He knew this chance meeting must have caught Rose by surprise. But amazingly, Rose conducted herself in the utmost professional manner, despite the blow she had just been handed.

"Oh wow, you already know my name. That's so cool," Stephanie told them. "You have no idea how excited I've been about this. I couldn't believe I'd been chosen. It's really good to meet you both. I'm sorry I was staring at you earlier, I saw the cameras and just assumed…"

Sometimes Rose forgot the camera around her neck. It had been a fixture in her life for so many years, almost like a weighted necklace. Rose always had it with her when she was working, and it occasionally seemed to disappear from her sight when she wasn't using it. But her camera was always there when she reached for it.

"Oh yeah, I guess the camera was a giveaway. It just sort of goes where I go. I forget that people associate me with it sometimes,"

Rose said, realizing the sudden introduction was quickly turning to awkward small talk.

"Frank and I are looking forward to getting to know you tonight at the rehearsal. Aren't we Frank?" Rose said, looking at him. She prayed he took the hint from her glance to either help keep the conversation going, or make polite excuses for them to move on.

"Absolutely. We're looking forward to getting to know you," Frank said. "We were just now headed to the ballroom to see how the decorating was coming along, and then to the wedding site to look at the lighting. We like to scout out everything early so we make the most of our time behind the lens."

Rose knew Frank was not only quick on his feet, but eloquent as well. She appreciated him taking the focus off her for a moment. There were some brides who gravitated to them as a team, and felt comfortable working with both of them equally. But some brides seemed to attach themselves only to Rose, simply because she was female. Of course Rose felt being female gave her no more expertise on being a bride than Frank. She had never been married and didn't know when or if she ever would. She had never tried on a wedding dress or an engagement ring, and certainly had never, ever, scribbled her name on a piece of paper changing her last name to that of a man's last name.

Rose didn't think that way. For her, being happy and content in life was something completely separate from falling in love. Her career already fulfilled her. A man in her life would be icing on the cake, so to speak. Rose found it ironic that this particular bride was clinging to her more than Frank. Say it wasn't so. Why did Trevor's fiancée have to like her? Of course she knew why she had a difficult time enjoying Stephanie's company in return. Or so she thought.

Stephanie continued to talk, and followed them as they walked to the ballroom. Only the beginning stages of the decoration process had gotten underway. And with the summer heat hanging thick in the air, most of it would need to wait until the last possible moment. Especially the parts that involved fresh flowers.

"This is where we'll have our reception, and the waterfall is out this way. Have you seen it yet, Rose? Or, is it Mrs. Millican?"

"It's Ms. Millican, or Miss if you prefer, but I'd rather you just call me Rose. And we've actually been at the hotel since yesterday, so we've already seen the grounds area. It's all part of being ready to get behind the lens, just like Frank told you."

"I'm sorry, I must be boring you both to tears," Stephanie said. "My fiancé's name is Trevor, but I guess if you guys knew my name, you probably knew his name as well, huh?"

"Actually, yes, we did. And Trevor is a friend of mine from high school."

Well, that wasn't technically true. He was a friend, and they did go to high school together. Rose merely left out a few details...like how and how well she and Trevor knew one another.

"Oh, wow, I didn't know. So is that how we got picked for this magazine thing?"

This magazine thing? Well, Rose wasn't altogether impressed with the vocabulary of one Miss Stephanie Ryder, but she tried to reserve judgment.

"No, my knowing Trevor had nothing at all to do with it, in fact. I had no idea until a few days ago the wedding even involved Trevor. It was a total surprise to me as well."

"Oh cool. Well, either way, I wouldn't have really cared. There's been a lot going on lately. His dad just died a couple of weeks ago, so the wedding plans have been real strange."

"Yes, our condolences to your and Trevor's families, Stephanie. We're both very sorry."

"Aw, thanks. When I first realized how sick he was, I was just afraid he would die in the middle of our wedding or something and keep this whole contest thing from happening. It was really too bad, but at least it's already over with."

Who was this completely unpolished girl and how could she possibly be who Trevor would spend the rest of his life with? Her vocabulary was so juvenile, and she just seemed to say the first words that entered her mind without investing a single thought in how they would sound before they left her mouth. Trevor had never gone to college, but he was knowledgeable in many ways, carried on witty and interesting conversation, and was ever so enjoyable in public. People loved him. Formal education wasn't a requirement for Rose to be impressed with someone or partial to their company, but a basic knowledge and understanding of social graces certainly was. She always tried to find the good in everyone. But right now, even good-hearted Rose was having a difficult time locating any redeemable qualities in Stephanie.

Frank looked over at Rose's contorted face. He rushed in to rescue the conversation before Rose did or said something she might later regret.

"Well, again, we're very sorry for your loss," Frank said, before any more could be said on the subject.

"I'm sure you have lots to do before tonight, Stephanie, and Rose and I are headed back to our room. But we'll see you back at the rehearsal."

"Yeah, I guess I have things to do. And Trevor was supposed to bring me lunch. I guess I'll go up to my room and sit and wait on him. He's often late when he brings me things like that. Goofy man."

Frank put his hand on Rose's back, and pressed a little firmly in order to get her attention. When she looked up at him, Frank shook his head back and forth as if to say, *no Rose, don't*. Rose gave him the angriest look he had ever seen on a woman's face. Somehow though, Frank managed to hand gesture enough so Rose knew what he was thinking.

"And so we look forward to seeing you back here at 5:00 p.m., is it?"

"Yeah, I think it's 5:00 p.m.. Knowing Trevor, he'll be late. I can hardly get him to do anything right. But I'll yell at him this afternoon and make sure he knows better."

"We can address the wedding party tonight, Stephanie, and make sure everyone knows the proper times to be exactly where they're supposed to be."

"Well, alright then. I'll spare yelling at him just this once. I'll see you guys tonight." And she just turned around and walked away -

without a proper goodbye or even a, *Nice to meet you*. Rose was definitely not impressed.

"I must kill her, Frank. That's just the way it is. You can spring me from jail in the morning, but you know I must kill her."

"Well, Rose, now let's not get ahead of ourselves. I'm sure you could just beat her up and leave her for dead somewhere and work out your frustrations without actually having to kill her."

"You know, you're right. Good idea."

"Rose, I was kidding! Down, girl."

"Oh hell, Frank. What the hell is her problem? I mean, seriously. I know you love me, and you know I care about Trevor, but come on. She must have fallen off some truck carrying farm animals that drove through town and hit a bump in the road."

"Rose! I've never heard you like this. You're cracking me up."

"Have you ever seen anything like her? Frank, the woman clearly left all her manners at home. Or somewhere. But you convince me she brought any manners at all with her here and I'll eat my own shoes for dinner tonight."

"Okay, okay. She clearly did not bring her manners with her today. And I've only met Trevor once for a few minutes. But if he was attracted to a woman like you, then the man either clearly likes a broad range of women, or else he's blind when he's with her. Oh, and deaf."

"See," Rose said, "you think it too, don't you? Ha! I never expected her to be perfect, but I did expect her to be a little more…"

"A little more like you, Rose?"

"Well, yes. More like me. Sure, why not? He could do worse. And apparently he's about to. You might as well just give me a few more minutes to rant because I'm not done yet. I have no idea why he would choose someone like her. She doesn't compliment him at all. And she seems quite rude, among other things," Rose went on. "I thought he had better taste, Frank. Shoot me, but I think he could have done better."

Rose took a few deep breaths, and realized this actually was not her business. Trevor had chosen this woman, but she wasn't anything like Rose. She couldn't decide if that was good or bad. So, confused and frustrated, Rose allowed Frank to get her a cold bottle of sparkling water, and they walked back towards the elevator. As the doors opened, they stepped inside and watched the doors close in front of them. Rose took a long, slow drink of her water. She also took a few more deep breaths.

"I'm sorry, Frank."

"Well, truthfully, I can see why it upset you a little, Rose. But maybe *she* is who *he* really is. Maybe you make him into someone different when he's with you, but someone he wouldn't otherwise be."

"Frank, that's really deep. I'm far too frustrated to have noticed anything so rational or said anything so eloquent myself right now. Why are you always so level-headed and well-spoken?"

"Maybe it's you, Rose. Maybe *you* are who *I* really am. And maybe you make me into someone I like and really was meant to be."

"I'd be a fool to walk away from you, Frank. Please don't ever let me be foolish."

The elevator doors opened, and Rose began to walk back to her room with Frank. She felt much better about who she was, but she wasn't proud of how she had acted in front of Frank.

"Frank, I'm sorry about the rant. I want you to make me a better me."

"My sweet, I love you just the way you are. You entertained the hell out of me downstairs a few minutes ago. Mind you, it's not always healthy to have that sort of attitude, especially in a professional situation. But, you managed to conduct yourself accordingly. As long as you have a mostly positive outlook and behave properly when you need to, and you're not angry at *me*...I see no problem with the occasional wordy outburst."

"I hope you're serious, because you might just not have heard the last of me this weekend."

Frank and Rose decided to order some snacks from room service and enjoy their view from the balcony while they worked that afternoon. They would mostly just mingle with the family and watch the wedding party at the rehearsal that evening. The real work would come tomorrow. Aside from the stress of this one particular wedding and its ultra-complicated situations, Frank had actually enjoyed his time away from the office with Rose. He wasn't sure if he was ready to go back to the confines of the business atmosphere just yet. The past few weeks away had meant a great deal to him. They had been in almost constant company of one another, but Frank didn't hate it. In fact, he loved it. Almost as much as he loved Rose.

Fortunately for everyone, the wedding rehearsal was fairly uneventful. Rose and Frank were already familiar with the hotel and after seeing five other weddings in the past five weeks, they felt more than prepared for yet one more. They decided to only stay a few minutes and excused themselves from the wedding party by saying they had preparations to make for tomorrow's event. Rose knew it was a lie when she said it, and Frank backed her up. As she expected, no one else seemed any the wiser. Rose had done her best to not make eye contact with Trevor and she had already seen quite enough of Stephanie. Frank took Rose to their room and held her until she fell asleep. They both needed their rest, and though they thought this last wedding would be the easiest, it would prove their most challenging to date.

Rose was awakened the next morning by the annoying noise of her cell phone buzzing. There were already multiple text messages from Trevor. Rose responded to him.

*"Trevor, I just woke up."*

His text response was almost immediate.

*"Rose, I need to see you. Now. Please. My time is running out."*

Frank knew what was about to happen. And he hated it. But it was inevitable. And if he loved Rose, he had to let it happen. She got out of bed with no words and got dressed.

"Somewhere to go, love?"

"Frank..."

"It's okay, Rose. Go."

She wanted to kiss him before she left, but it felt awkward. It felt wrong, and she knew it was. She was leaving this good and decent man in her bed for a man she knew was getting married in a few hours. Rose had never thought lower of herself. And yet, she walked out the door and down the long and winding hall to the room where she would finally be alone again with Trevor.

## CHAPTER SIXTEEN

Rose wasn't quite sure what to expect. She nervously walked up to his door, and before she could knock, the door opened. How he knew she was standing there Rose didn't understand, but it was apparent they both felt the need to kiss and touch and love at least one more time. And if the moment spoke to both of them, maybe it wouldn't be the last time.

"Rose, you came. It feels like it's been forever since I've really been able to hold you," Trevor said as he took her hand and pulled her into his room. "Thank you for agreeing to meet me. I know it's risky, and confusing, too." He quickly looked up and down the hall before closing the door, just to make sure no one saw them.

"I'm terribly confused, Trevor." Still at a loss for words, Rose sat down on the bed. Trevor sat down beside her.

"What is it, Rose?"

She didn't answer. It was just one of those times when she couldn't speak. Inside, she knew the words, but they weren't leaving her mouth, so Trevor had no idea what she was thinking.

Rose tried and tried to speak, grasping for any words to say, but the words just weren't there. All she could do was react. She reached for Trevor's hand, and traced every part of it with her own hand. Their fingers interlocked. She brought his hand up next to her cheek and closed her eyes, as if she were absorbing how it felt. As though she would carry it with her forever. She pulled it away from her cheek to kiss it, ever so slowly, then moved it to her neck and guided his touch around her chest, breasts, then down to her hips. She did it intentionally. She knew once his hands felt her body that he wouldn't allow her to leave. Anyway, she wanted to stay.

Rose watched as Trevor gave in to her suggestions. His mind might have tried to fight it in the slightest way, but his body was far from willing to watch her leave. They wanted each other. Rose felt somewhere deep inside that she might regret making love to this man on the day when he was about to marry someone else. But right now, for these few more moments, he was hers. She had one more chance to find out how he truly felt, just like Frank said. She knew if Trevor loved her then she would see it in his eyes. And she wanted to show him how she felt, with her lips, her hands, her whole body. And though she sensed from the minute she first touched him that it wouldn't stop his wedding, she continued.

She could feel herself sliding back into that familiar spot in Trevor's arms, where she had been before, and where she had dreamed about returning. Being next to his very breath again was like coming home. She buried her nose into his neck and his chest, remembering the way his skin felt, the way he smelled. Everything about him seemed to belong to her at that second. Rose had already shared so much with this man. Love and laughter, sex and tears. Yet, here they were now, with what they both feared was a final goodbye.

Neither of them spoke it aloud, but when their eyes met, it was clear they both knew. Trevor was locked into the relationship with Stephanie. He would remain in that small town where he just took over his father's store. He couldn't leave there for Rose, and Rose could never go back there, not even for him. She was certain they would both attempt to concoct some solution for meeting in the future, but it would never transpire. The rest of their forever was right in front of them in the next hour or two. Right now was all they had.

"I'm really sorry," Trevor told her, with a face full of sincerity. "I'm so very sorry, Rose. I don't know how all this happened. I thought I had my life figured out. Well, part of it got figured out for me, with the store and all, but that's okay. I can deal with that. I knew *that* would eventually happen to me. But, Rose…I never knew *you* would happen to me."

Rose stood up beside the bed, took Trevor's face and held it close to her chest. She longed to give him comfort in this impossible situation. She didn't know *he* would happen to her either, and neither of them deserved to have their hearts broken like this. With his face in her hands, Rose invested all she had into the kiss she rested on his lips. A kiss which said everything from *I'm glad we had this* to *I'm sorry it all had to end this way*. Rose never saw herself as the kind of woman who would be found in the bed of a man on his wedding day to another woman, but these were unforeseen circumstances.

Every touch was precious, and beautiful, and sad, but they did the best they could. They slowly helped each other remove their clothes, one article at a time. Rose remained standing in front of Trevor, who was still sitting on the edge of the bed, and they never stopped looking at one another, not for a single second. She didn't want to forget his eyes or his face. Every time she closed her eyes right now, either in ecstasy or in tears, was one second less she had to leave a lasting picture in her mind. Ever the photographer, but without a camera this time. These were pictures no one else would ever be able to find. They would only exist within her memory. They would only belong to Rose.

When all the clothes had been removed from their bodies and tossed out of the way, Rose slowly sat down across his lap. She wrapped her legs around him, and locked her feet together behind his back as she felt him push inside her. She didn't want any of it to end, though she knew it eventually would. So she wanted to live out this moment like no other. This wasn't the hot and passionate time on the desk. This was very different. This was about memorizing a touch, the shape of his nose, the way her lips felt on his earlobe and his neck, the strength and the gentleness in the way his hands held onto her back, the feeling she couldn't deny felt so perfect when they were completely connected. She wanted it to last forever, but time would not permit them such a luxury. And so, as their time together culminated, she heard him whisper in her ear, "I'll always love you, Rose. No matter what." She clenched her teeth together and held back the tears. This was no time for sadness. She still had a few moments to share with him and crying wasn't the way she wanted to remember them.

"I'll always love you too, Trevor. Please remember that."

They continued to kiss, and finally lay back on the bed together, exhausted from exposing their bodies and souls to one another so openly and completely. Without realizing it, they had fallen asleep in one another's arms. When Rose awoke, she shuddered at the idea she had allowed herself to sleep on such a crucial day when she was expected to work. Thankfully, what had seemed like an entire night's sleep had only been about a twenty minute nap, and Rose knew she must leave Trevor in this room, once and for all. This had been their last time, but she didn't want to wake him to say goodbye all over again. They'd had too many goodbyes in their short time together already.

As Rose quietly tiptoed across the carpeted floor, gathering her clothes and getting dressed again, she watched Trevor sleeping there on the bed. If things had happened differently, he could have been the husband she would find napping in their own bed one day. Or falling asleep after a football game on the couch. Or resting with a newborn baby - their baby - on his chest as they slept. Maybe, if things had been different. But they weren't. And now, they never would be. She wanted to leave a note, but if anyone else came in the room and found it, all could go to hell quickly. She didn't want that for him. She couldn't leave a trace. She would text him when she arrived back at her own room. That way, he would be the only one to see the message. After all, he had a wedding to get dressed for, and he might need the text to awaken him from his nap. She left this beautiful sleeping man in this bed all alone. As much as she wanted him, he wasn't meant to be hers.

He really *wasn't* meant to be hers. She didn't want to admit it to herself, and especially not to Frank, but she *had* seen that same look in Trevor's eyes. The exact same look she had seen in Frank's eyes that night when he made love to her on the balcony. The look Frank said he didn't think she would find in Trevor's eyes. But alas, she indeed had. She saw the same lust. She saw the same desire. And above all, she saw love. It wasn't exactly the same kind of love that Frank had for her, but they were different people. They loved her in different ways, and she loved them in two completely different ways. And though Rose and Trevor cared greatly for one another now, and had once shared a common background, their worlds could never align, and Rose knew it. Maybe if she had known him better, sooner. Maybe if they had spoken that day they saw each other in town just before Rose had left for college. Maybe if he had said hello that day in the cafeteria when she dropped her book and he picked it up for her, but only walked away with a smile. Fate had been cruel to any possibility of their future together, and they would learn to live with the memory of what was, and what might have been.

With tears in her eyes now, she blew him a kiss, and quietly, and a little reluctantly, left the room. She cried all the way down the long and winding hall to the elevator, and prayed no one else would see her face so red from all the tears. Thankfully, her ride was not interrupted. She arrived on her own floor and ran down the hall to her room. As she fumbled for the card key in her pocket, she saw the hotel room door open in front of her. There stood Frank, waiting on her with open arms.

"Come here, love."

He only needed to see her for a moment to know exactly what had happened. He had known it from the beginning. There was nothing to forgive, because Frank didn't blame her for anything. He took her into his arms, and held her softly, running his hands up and down her back. He took a chance, he supposed, allowing her to go to Trevor, but he had to let her go. If he had kept her from him, she'd have always wondered what might have been.

She looked up at Frank, not wanting to admit what had happened. He kissed her lips anyhow, knowing where they had just been. And he held her close anyway, knowing whose hands had just held her.

"Are you okay, Rose? Do you want me to shoot the wedding without you? I will, and I won't say a word to Jeannie if that's what has to happen."

"Why would anyone love me this much, Frank, the way you do? I don't deserve it. I don't deserve you. You've been ever so patient with me this whole time. You've watched me bounce back and forth in my decision making. You knew all along I'd end up with Trevor one more time before his wedding. I'm sorry, I tried not to, but making love with him was the only way I knew how to say goodbye. I wouldn't blame you if you slammed this door in my face right now and made me go find my own room. You would be completely within your rights."

Still standing in the open doorway after their long embrace, Frank pulled her inside the room where they could speak in private.

"Sure, I knew you would go to him, Rose. And do you know why I knew? Because you're an emotional and beautiful person, inside and out. If I heard that another woman did what you did, I might think less of her. But you, Rose…well, I've known you a while. And I've watched you. If Trevor meant anything at all to you, then a quick goodbye would have never sufficed. You give all of yourself to whatever you do…your friendships, your career, your relationships. Everything."

"But I have a relationship with you too, Frank."

"Yes, you do, Rose, always and forever. If you want it."

"I love you, Frank. And I feel so terribly embarrassed that you know what I did today. It's almost like you knew it would happen even before I did though. You really love me. Don't you? I mean, beyond the physical, beyond the career we share, and with all my flaws and mistakes and things I do that drive you crazy. You love it all. And you did know before I even knew. I can tell. You even knew it wouldn't work out with Trevor, too. Didn't you, Frank?"

"Well, I hoped. He didn't have that same look in his eyes, did he, Rose? It wasn't there. You really did look at him just like I asked you to, and you didn't find it."

This was the one secret Rose would keep from Frank…this man who loved her completely. It would be the only secret she'd ever had from him. But she couldn't possibly tell him that she *did* see that look in Trevor's eyes. She merely knew their lives would never line up enough for it to matter.

"It was all really lovely, Frank. Like a movie or something. But to answer your question, no. It just wasn't there. It hurt to think that we could have all that, well, you know, physically. And I looked for that sincerity, that hint or clue, that sparkle like you had in your eyes with me that night on the balcony. I felt things, Frank. But I realize now, it was just two people with chemistry telling each other goodbye."

Rose wasn't sure if the most difficult part of the conversation was lying to Frank, or realizing the disappointment in herself as she listened to the lies coming out of her own mouth. She loved Trevor.

She always would. But it wasn't going to work with him, and she could never hurt Frank. She felt like she might be sick to her stomach, but there was just no time for such a thing.

"Are you okay, Rose? Do you want to tell me the rest of what happened?"

"Well, we fell asleep for a few minutes afterwards," Rose began to explain. "When I awoke, I was so afraid I had been asleep longer than I actually had. I silently gathered my clothes, blew him a kiss from across the room, and walked out. I guess blowing the kiss was more for me than him, since he wasn't even awake to see it. I bawled out loud after I shut the door behind me, but I left without talking to him. Without even saying goodbye. I was going to text him when I got back here just to make certain he woke up so he could get ready for tonight."

"So, you were together, and you left him asleep, and you still want him to go through with his wedding to someone else tonight?" Frank asked her. "Is that what I just understood you to say?"

"Well, yes," Rose answered truthfully. "Yes, that's what I said. And I stand by it. I do want him to go through with his wedding tonight. I do."

"You know, Rose, I adore you as a friend, and even more as a lover. But those sure are words that I'd love to hear you say to me one day."

"What words, Frank?"

"*I do*. I'd love to hear you say the words *I do* to me one day. But let's get through today first. You making love with him was merely your way of saying goodbye. I understand it, because I understand you. I know it must have been special."

Rose felt so very embarrassed, and felt warm and flush in Frank's presence.

"Frank, how can you say that?"

"Because I know you. You're not the kind of woman who could give yourself to someone unless you really loved them. Maybe Trevor doesn't care for you as much as you care for him. Actually, Rose, forgive me if I'm saying too much, but you love so deeply, on such an intense level. I don't know that Trevor is capable of returning the magnitude of love to you that you deserve."

Frank took a break in the heavy conversation to study Rose's face. He took his right index finger, and tilted her chin upward so he could see into her eyes. Frank believed that the eyes were truly the window to one's soul, and Rose was one of the few people he had ever allowed to look into his own soul. He wanted to look back into her eyes now as he asked her a very important question.

"Are you sure you can do this tonight? My offer still stands to let you out of it, if you like."

"I do *not* like. I committed to shoot six weddings with you and, by damn, I'm not stopping at five. Never mind my drama. I made a commitment to you and to the magazine and one way or another, I'll be just fine. All in all, it will probably be therapeutic to see them exchange vows for myself. I can move forward with my life now and know what we shared was a connection which wasn't meant to last forever. I'll be a better person for seeing the wedding. I won't say it will be the easiest thing I've ever done though."

Frank stepped away from her and walked into the bathroom. He turned on the shower water, and she could see the steam begin to rise and cloud the mirror.

"You like really hot showers. Don't you, my dear?"

"You know I do."

"Well, here's your hot shower. If you hurry, we can still make it downstairs right on schedule. And if you need a few minutes, I'll go downstairs and cover things until you get there."

"Frank, one more thing."

"Yes? What is it, my sweet Rose?"

"You really are the best person I've ever known." It was possibly the most sincere statement she had ever made. To anyone. And certainly the most humble of any words she had ever spoken.

He kissed her sweetly on the nose, once quickly on the lips, and then hastened her into the bathroom to prepare for the evening. Frank knew there was only one way to handle things tonight, and now that he knew just where Rose stood with him, he needed a few minutes alone to begin making his plans.

## CHAPTER SEVENTEEN

As Rose stepped into the steamy shower, she thought of coming home from Lily's funeral, and how the shower seemed to have saved her that night. She needed that same sort of magic this afternoon. As the shower water to fell over her like a hot rain, she once again washed Trevor from her body. This would be an evening filled with many different types of emotion. To call it a challenging evening would be an understatement. But Rose thought she could do it. Actually, she had to do it. After all, this was business. This was for her career. As much of a chore as it would be, Rose had to remind herself this was just another day on the job. Another bride, another groom, another wedding, just like they had done for the past five weeks. More faces to capture, more dresses to show in detail, more venues to showcase. There would be vows, cake, and dancing like all the others. Only this wedding would have Trevor and Stephanie, too.

After the shower, after the pre-game locker room pep talk she had with herself silently while the water ran over her body, after she felt her thoughts and emotions were collected enough to move on with the rest of the day, she turned off the water and stepped out of the shower. Rose heard Frank rustling around through his luggage in the room, and she swore she heard words as well. She tried to make sure she was quiet in case he was on the phone. She opened the door and peeked out into the room. The cold air of the hotel room hit her quickly as the steam escaped from the bathroom.

"Frank, you there?" Rose whispered.

"Yeah, Rose. Right here, baby. Do you need something?"

"No, I just heard, well, I thought I heard you talking to someone, either at the door or maybe on the phone. Just thought I heard voices."

"Just me, baby. I might have been talking to myself. I do that sometimes, but it's just because I'm a little odd."

"You're not odd, Frank. You're the coolest guy I know. Now, I might occasionally refer to you as eccentric."

"Eccentric, huh? Okay, I'll accept that. So long as you don't think it's a bad thing."

"Never."

Frank smiled as she ran back to the bathroom. She looked so much happier for having been with Trevor one more time and finally understanding what it all truly meant. Except for the first night Frank was with her, Rose had been battling feelings for Trevor in her head and in her heart their entire time together. The idea she might finally be dealing with those feelings made Frank feel hopeful about his standing with Rose now. He thought it sounded delightful – the idea that she might not be carrying around an invisible third person in the middle of their relationship any longer. Of course, it wasn't as simple for Rose as he thought.

Frank looked at his watch and saw they still had around two hours before they needed to go downstairs. And although he didn't want to push Rose, he had hoped they would be able to go sooner. Frank knew there were too many characters in the play tonight, and it was only flirting with disaster to take a chance on arriving even five minutes later than scheduled. He heard Rose in the bathroom, drying her hair and making progress in readying herself for the evening. As he listened to her, he couldn't help but think to himself that she was a hell of a girl. Just a hell of a girl.

As Frank was admiring her in his mind, Rose silently stepped out of the bathroom. Her hair was dried, but not too much else seemed to have been accomplished. Frank wanted to kindly intervene in order to quicken her pace.

"Rose, sweetie, I know our itinerary has us arriving downstairs at 3:00, but I was hoping we could get there around 2:45. There's just a number of, extenuating circumstances, shall we say, which make me want to know for certain that all is well. Is that a problem for you, dear?"

"Well, no, it shouldn't be. I just need to pick out something to wear. Hmmm…what to wear."

Rose stared blankly at her luggage. Her clothes were scattered everywhere. Meanwhile, Frank's clothes were neatly stacked and folded, with clean clothes on one side of the suitcase and dirty clothes on the other. Of course, women always had more layers and accessories. Rose had many different moods, and she dressed accordingly. Frank had shirts, pants, belts, socks and shoes. That was about it for a guy. But she loved being a girl. And sometimes she was a very messy one.

Rose rummaged through her suitcase to find just the right thing to wear. She always dressed for comfort on the day of a big photo shoot. But today, she needed to blend sophistication and style, comfort and professionalism, and just plain old-fashioned pretty. She looked up to the ceiling, realizing she had been so tangled and torn with her feelings for these two very different men, she had not allowed herself to feel Lily's spirit around her in a while. Silently and only to herself, Rose looked up to the ceiling and pleaded with Lily.

*If you've ever really been near me since you died – if you've ever really been in my presence at all since the day I lost you, I beg you to please be my angel today. If you were alive, I know you would be here for me in person, but you're out there somewhere, and I can't see you or touch you. But still, somehow, you've never really left me. I just know it. Lily, please, this may be the one day in my life when I've needed you the most. And I need you for everything today - from telling me what to wear to telling me this will all be okay. Please let me feel you today, Lily. I miss you so very much.*

Frank looked on as Rose stared at the ceiling. She had not shared with him that she felt Lily was still with her. He dared not interrupt her what he suspected was Rose having a conversation with Lily. She finally looked back to her suitcase, mounded with her collection of clothes.

"I know I'm not as great as Lily at helping pick out clothes, but I could try. I actually think you look good in all of them."

Rose looked stunned as she glanced over at Frank.

"How did you know that I was talking to Lily? How could you possibly know that?"

"Just a hunch. I never knew her, but I know you. I love you. I love how your mind works. The way you stared at your clothes and then stared at the ceiling. I just thought…"

"Why on earth do you find any redeeming qualities in me? I am just such a mess, and you love me through it all."

Rose realized Frank knew her better than anyone. And he loved her more than anyone. Her soul still felt a bit bruised from all she had been through that day, but being in the presence of this amazing man was surely one of Lily's gifts. He had, after all, been there from the moment she heard of Lily's passing.

Frank walked over to her suitcase and picked up a skirt and a blouse. He knew nothing of fashion *per se*, and he knew Rose normally did photo shoots in pants. But he also knew she needed to feel her very best today, and she loved the way she felt in skirts and dresses. He merely selected something he had seen her wear before and handed it to her.

"My dear, you're the best mess that's ever happened to me. Now let's get ready to go downstairs. It will be okay, Rose. I promise. I'll be there with you. And Lily will be with you there, too."

Rose suddenly felt empowered after hearing what Frank said to her. It was all perfect. Even down to the clothing selection Frank had made for her, even if it was just a random accident. She got dressed, finished her hair and makeup, and walked to the mirror to give herself the once over. Rose was quite pleased with Frank's choice…a soft cotton beige top, just a little low-cut, with a ruffle circling the entire neckline, and a black cotton knee-length a-lined skirt. It was simple and understated. She felt pretty. She also felt ready for this challenge. She slipped on her black pumps, picked up her camera and placed it around her neck. Her camera was always the quintessential fashion accessory, especially on *game day* as she sometimes thought of days like today.

"You look stunning. Just stunning."

"You silly man. Just comfortable clothes that hold up well for a gig like this. Stunning isn't quite the right word."

"Well, I stand by it. I said stunning and I meant it."

Frank picked up his camera and followed Rose to the door. He felt as though he had done well helping her transition from her time with Trevor earlier to her professional headspace for the evening's activities. He didn't want any credit for it, he simply wanted to take this beautiful woman all the places she deserved to go. She deserved to pull herself back together, and look great, and shoot this wedding tonight as she normally would have. Rose thought Frank made her strong, but Frank just helped her along. He believed in her, even when she didn't believe in herself. He was the one person who knew she was strong, all on her own.

Rose put her hand on the door handle to leave the room. She stopped and turned back to the door to face Frank.

"Kiss me," she said, looking up at him like a helpless little girl.

Without a word, Frank started to embrace her, and they suddenly realized they both had their cameras around their necks. It didn't make for a very close embrace, and they laughed together. Frank moved his camera to his side for a moment, and Rose did the same. He pressed his body close to her. Very close. And he softly kissed her. He then took just a moment to rest his face in her neck, breathing in her sweet cologne and touching her soft hair. But he didn't want her to arrive downstairs looking as though she had just had an afternoon romp, and he was careful to not get too excited himself either.

"Wow. I guess we better go on downstairs. But…thank you," she said with a smile that almost made him melt onto the floor. She finally opened the door, and he followed her downstairs. Though he would have followed her anywhere.

They arrived in the lobby precisely at 2:45 p.m., just as Frank had hoped. Now the challenge was to make certain the remainder of the evening went as smoothly as possible. Frank wasn't so sure about that, but he had plans of his own, plans not related to the wedding. Frank was the only one who knew though, and this was the one thing he couldn't share with Rose. Not just yet.

They made their way down the corridor towards the area of the wedding and reception. Somehow, through being so preoccupied with herself, and Trevor, and Frank, and getting ready, she had not bothered to look outside. It wasn't until she approached the door leading out to the waterfall that she realized the color of the sky, and she stopped dead in her tracks. It didn't look like a storm, but more like a soft summer rain was most likely on its way. Rose had seen these many times growing up nearby and, most recently, on the morning of Lily's funeral. She had accepted the fact that there would be a wedding, but she had already decided in her head there would be no more surprises. Rose just wasn't sure if she had the strength to jump unexpected hurdles. And please, no rain. Not today.

She looked at Frank and without speaking, he knew exactly what she was thinking.

"Rose, hang on. I'm sure the hotel has alternate arrangements. I'll go talk to the coordinator and see what they've come up with. I know you didn't want any surprises today, but just hang on, okay? Remember what I told you? It will be okay." And he squeezed her hand tightly as he walked away.

Meanwhile, Rose stepped outside toward the waterfall and saw no sign of decorations. It was as though someone had forgotten it was all supposed to take place. It could have meant they were waiting to see if the inclement weather passed by, or that they had already decided to change the venue for the ceremony. Rose just needed to know one way or the other so she could begin to process the deviations in the schedule. She really wasn't the kind of gal who liked deviations in schedules. Especially not today.

When she walked around the corner, she saw all the white wooden folding chairs for guest seating. They were still stacked inside the hotel, along with a white metal archway and a white aisle runner which was rolled tightly and leaned against the wall. Fresh rose petals for the flower girl waited in a white basket. Each of the items just sat there, waiting on a decision from Mother Nature as to how and where and when exactly they would be used. How fragile it all was, Rose thought to herself. Someone could wait their whole life for one day. After choosing one single person, and after months and months of spending and selecting and planning, and it could still all be turned upside down at the last minute because of a change in weather.

It just didn't seem fair, and it wasn't even Rose's wedding. And though she didn't care for Stephanie in the slightest, she had a soft spot for every single bride she had met the past few weeks. Weddings no longer seemed cliché and hokey to her. She had seen good people - real people - pledging their love and with whatever money and resources they had, throw a celebration with family, friends and the ones they loved that they would always remember. And for the first time in a long time, maybe ever, and certainly long after many other friends her same age, Rose finally began to fall in love with the idea of falling in love.

She looked up just as Frank came walking back with the wedding coordinator. They seemed quite conversive and Rose was curious what news they had. The pretty woman who accompanied Frank extended her hand to Rose and introduced herself.

"Hi, Rose, I'm Mindy, the wedding coordinator. And a big fan of the magazine, by the way," she said, shaking Rose's hand up and down, again and again. Rose was always pleased when a reader expressed their enjoyment of the magazine, and she had grown more comfortable with time about talking to people personally. In her early days at the magazine, it was all about being behind the lens, but this promotional assignment had taught Rose that there was a balance of interacting with people as well as photographing them.

"Thank you, Mindy. It's great to meet you. So, what's the situation with the weather and the ceremony?" Rose asked anxiously.

"Well, we're trying to give it until the last possible minute. The weather is iffy, and the chance of rain is off and on for the rest of the afternoon. It's just about impossible to predict what will happen now, so we will just have everything ready and waiting. If we're ninety minutes out and the weather isn't cooperating, then we will move it inside to one of our other ballrooms, just adjacent to the reception site. Otherwise, the bride wishes us to take our chances and have it outside."

Of course she did, Rose thought to herself. Why didn't she just give everyone big tarps to hold over their heads while she walked down the aisle? Hell, maybe she had big white rain boots...who knew? But Rose had to stay focused. And she didn't need to be distracted by Stephanie. She just needed the wedding to take place somewhere and for it to be tasteful.

Mindy was one of those ladies who moved quickly, and never stood still for very long. She promised to let one of the them know as soon as she knew a definitive answer. As she disappeared like a little wedding fairy, they found themselves alone again contemplating the evening and what it might hold.

"Okay, Frank, just please tell me this will still be tasteful. I see it won't go off without a hitch as I might have dreamed, so I'll settle for the next best thing, which is for it not to end up a complete and utter disaster. If the ceremony is moved to an indoor venue, it might change the tone of the whole evening. This was supposed to be an outdoor wedding! Frank, your thoughts?"

Rose finally finished, though Frank wasn't completely certain, so he waited a moment before speaking.

"Look, we'll get around this. We'll take shots outside the hotel, even if it has to be tomorrow, and we'll do what we can. Sure, the grounds here are lovely, but the entire inside of this place is gorgeous as well. I'm sure if it has to be moved inside it will still be lovely. Alright?" he concluded, rubbing her back with his hand, and dying to divulge his secret to her. Still, there was much left yet to do and he was her partner right now, not her lover. So, it was business before pleasure.

They agreed to split up and take indoor pictures for a while. Stephanie's mother, a little older and a lot more old-fashioned, had insisted the bride and groom not see each other before the ceremony. And so, sticking with the old-fashioned theme, Frank went to take pictures of the males in the wedding party - the groomsmen and the groom. Meanwhile, Rose (yawn) went to take photos of the females - the uptight mother, the bridesmaids (she could only imagine if they were friends of Stephanie's) and the bride. Ah, yes, the bride. Well, Rose didn't want to go there right now. But, alas, she had to. And so, like the professional she was, she did. She took a big gulp, swallowed her pride, and began walking.

## CHAPTER EIGHTEEN

Rose arrived at the area where the bridal party were readying themselves for the ceremony. She knocked, declared her name so as not to surprise anyone, and opened the door. There stood some very lovely bridesmaids. And to her surprise and relief, they were elegant and poised with some of the most beautiful gowns she had seen in the six weeks of travel. Hair, makeup, nails, jewelry, and shoes - all to perfection and most tastefully done. She introduced herself to the bridesmaids, and each was more excited than the one before to shake her hand and have her photograph them. The ladies had obviously outdone themselves for the magazine, and Rose almost immediately began to feel more at ease. Even the uptight mother of the bride was not so daunting as she had envisioned, and everyone almost seemed more excited about meeting Rose than about the wedding itself. And, just when Rose felt more relaxed and found her camera giving her the easiest workout it had experienced in recent weeks, Stephanie walked in. Rose had imagined a bride without an impressive amount of class or taste, making an entrance without grace or elegance. But this was a lovely bride, ready to be married – and in style. This was a bride who brought her A-game. At least it appeared so and that's what mattered to Rose. This woman had no idea that just hours ago, Rose had been intimate with her soon-to-be husband. Overwhelming didn't come close to describing the moment for Rose, but she took a deep breath, and held her camera like a familiar lover. Her camera was, after all, her first and truest love. Perhaps in the midst of all these recent complications, Rose had forgotten. And she didn't know it until today, but the camera would allow her to conquer the most absurd and seemingly impossible of situations.

"Stephanie, you look lovely," Rose said, almost hating the words as they left her mouth, but knowing it was too late to retract them. But it was true, and she knew it. It was only then that Rose actually ever thought she wanted to wear one of those damn itchy, heavy, expensive collections of lace and netting one day. Maybe. But Rose could finally, almost, imagine herself preparing for such a day as this. Not quite, but almost.

"Thank you, Rose," Stephanie replied, politely and surprisingly well-spoken. And suddenly, Rose wondered if she had been falsely introduced to some horrible bridal imposter in the hall before, because this woman was very different. This wasn't at all who she thought Trevor was marrying. Not that it mattered what she thought, but for her own peace of mind, it seemed like the planets had aligned and the universe finally made sense again. She looked around at all these women, so perfectly coiffed. And especially Stephanie, so decorated and ready to be a bride. Trevor's bride.

Taking picture after picture, relieved she had united with her camera once again and lost herself in the moments of where she actually was, she felt a buzz in her pocket and reached down to check her cell phone. She saw a new message from Frank and excused herself from the bridal party to answer a message from her magazine partner.

When she looked at the message, the words halted her heartbeat. "Rose, I've made pictures of everyone here. Hell, I've made pictures of every male in the near vicinity. I've even made pictures of the tribute rose they have here in memory of his father. But Trevor himself is missing in action. Help."

Rose almost thought he was joking, but Frank wasn't a joking type…and especially not about this. He might be her lover now, but first, he was her mentor. And he was her mentor because he was a consummate professional. Frank would never joke about a situation like that. She texted him back to meet in the hall for a brief face to face conversation.

Rose excused herself from the dressing room, thanked them for their cooperation during the picture session, and said she would see them again soon. Rose remained calm while in their presence, though the minute the door shut, she was living in a world of panic. When she saw Frank in the hall, she lunged toward him, grasping his hands for support in some combination of a lover and a colleague.

"Frank, what's going on?"

"Rose, I have no idea. He's just not there. Everyone else is there but him. He's not answering phone calls or texts. He's not in his room and not in his car. I hate to ask you, I really do, but do you have any other ideas?"

"I was going to text him after I left him today to make sure he woke up, but I forgot. Though I guess if he was still asleep he would have been in his room. So if he's not in his room, and not in his car, and not where he should be right now….hmmm…" And then she had an idea.

As Rose removed her precious camera from around her neck and handed it off to Frank, she assured him she had an idea. If Rose was willing to part with her camera, it was surely for something very necessary. "Frank, trust me. I'm trusting you with my camera, so please, trust me. I'll be back as soon as I can. I'll text you with any news."

Rose turned and sprinted down the hall, but stopped and turned around to Frank once again. "Hey, I love you, you amazing man."

"Yeah, yeah, I love you, too. Now, get out of here and find the groom. Of all the weddings I've ever seen people make fun of, it's always about a runaway *bride*. But no sir. Not me. I get a runaway *groom*," Frank rambled under his breath as Rose sprinted down the hall.

"I owe you, Frank," Rose said, as she kept running. "I've got this one. Just trust me."

Rose thought as she ran. She told Frank she would handle it. And to trust her. But she honestly didn't have any idea exactly where he would be. She only thought it would be best to look for him herself. She knew him well. Where would a man such as Trevor be right now? She had to take a moment and allow herself to feel him again, in her heart, and in her mind. It was the only way she could find him. If neither his best friends nor his family knew where to look, she had to momentarily think of him as a lover. It seemed like the best possibility for locating him.

And then it hit her.

Rose immediately headed toward the hotel bar. And when she arrived, sure enough, there sat Trevor. Near the back of the bar at the very same two-seater table they shared after they had left Lily's wake. The place where they shared the cups of kindness in memory of Lily. Rose walked in slowly, so not to startle him. Although in his condition, it would have been extremely difficult to startle him.

There he sat, drinking far too much but looking better than she had ever seen him. She walked up to him and sat down in the chair opposite him.

"Well, so here you are," she said calmly. Rose had realized that Trevor might be thinking of her right now, and that he would be in a place where they once sat together. As she waited on him to answer, she sensed this might be a more difficult conversation than she actually wanted to have.

"Hey, baby. I figured a chick like you would know where to find me. You knew where I'd be, didn't you, Rose?" Trevor slurred, obviously under the influence.

"Trevor, what are you doing? You have an entire wedding party wondering where you are. Not to mention a bride in waiting who has no clue you are missing in action. Do you have any idea how much I'm covering for you right now? In fact, I even have someone covering for me." She motioned for the server to come to their table.

"Oh yeah, your friend Frank. Just how much of a *friend* is he now, Rose? Come on, you can tell me." Trevor slurred his words a bit more than he should, considering he was getting married in under three hours. Rose just looked down at her hands in her lap while Trevor continued, in a mangled sort of way. "I just thought I'd have a beer before the ceremony to loosen things up a bit."

"It looks as though you've had more than *a beer*, Trevor."

When the server came to their table Rose spoke over Trevor, who tried to order yet another beer. "Two coffees please, and put it on the tab for my room for *The Bride's Side* magazine." Thank goodness the server seemed to understand her mission.

"Certainly," the server replied, with a wink and a nod toward the would-be-groom. Damn it, this certainly wasn't anything Rose signed up for. How in the hell did she find herself in these situations?

"Trevor, what are you doing? You have a wedding and a bride waiting for you. Can I please ask what you are doing here?"

"I can't do it, Rose. I mean, I just don't think I can do it." And then Trevor left the table without another word and stumbled toward the restroom.

Rose took the opportunity to text Frank and let him know she had located Trevor, and he insisted on joining her there. It wasn't that he didn't think Rose could handle him on her own, but Frank had seen men in this situation before. And even though he knew Rose was an extraordinary lady, this wasn't necessarily a job for a lady.

Frank appeared almost immediately, and as Rose pleaded with him to leave, Trevor returned to the table. He fumbled as he sat down once again, and then he noticed Frank.

"Hey there. It's our good buddy, Frank. How the hell are you, Frank?" But Frank said nothing in return.

The server had acted quickly and delivered the coffees to their table. Rose thanked her, and then ducked her head when Trevor asked for some Irish Cream to go with it. But the server just laughed as she walked away without answering him.

"Trevor, this is a very desperate attempt to bring you back to earth just a little bit. We aren't having a drinking contest, we're here to wake you up enough so you can show up for your own wedding. You'll have your coffee straight, and definitely not with any liquor of any kind," Rose said without wavering.

"Did you hear that, Frank? Rose doesn't want me, so she's pushing me to go ahead and marry Stephanie. It's probably because you two are doing the deed, huh? Come on, Frank tell me. She's doin' you now, isn't she?"

Frank was restraining himself more than Rose had ever seen, but then he finally lunged towards Trevor. Frank was not quite as tall as Trevor, but he was well built and strong. She knew if he unleashed himself on Trevor it would be ugly, so she put her arm across his chest. Rose looked into Frank's eyes, deeply. Maybe deeper than she ever had. She whispered to him, "Frank, he's drunk. We're here to photograph his wedding. Remember, this is work."

Frank realized then that Rose was the wiser of them. She sat there, poised and confident, handling the emotions of two men who cared for her. She had learned from Frank to put professionalism first. She was here for business and, so, business-like she would be. She overcame her own personal emotions in order to gain control of an extremely difficult situation, and she had prevented Frank from making a crucial mistake as well.

Frank looked at Rose, who struggled with such a difficult moment. She had needed him so much today, and yet he had needed her this time. "Well played, lover. Well played."

She smiled back at him, as though she had been crowned Miss America. "Thanks, lover."

"See, you guys called each other lover. I knew you guys were doin' it," Trevor answered.

Frank knew at this point that Rose was in control of this situation. She was extraordinary, he thought to himself, and he kissed her on the head. He pointed his finger at Trevor like a strict parent and walked away, but kept his eye on him until he was out of view. Rose and Trevor sat at the table alone once again.

"Trevor. Get a hold of your damn self," Rose said to him sternly, and pushed his coffee cup towards him. "Drink your coffee and listen to me. You have a wedding to attend, and if I have to drag you there by your ear myself, then I will. You committed to this and I'm here to make pictures of you doing it. So get your ass up and get to your wedding."

He sat there, still sipping his coffee, and seemed only moderately shocked at Rose's words. It would soon be clear she had not had the kind of effect on him she had hoped. "But baby," he said as though he hadn't heard a word she said, "what about me and you? And why did you walk out on me today?"

Rose stood there fighting for the power and strength to conquer what would surely become a defining moment in her twenty-eight years. And so she pulled from within the ability to both remember and accomplish, to reflect and overcome, to think back on what they shared that was good, and use it to help them both move on.

"Trevor," she began, still signaling him to keep drinking his coffee, "I can't explain what happened between us. Nothing like that has ever happened to me. Ever. It wasn't necessarily perfect or meant to last forever, but it happened. And I liked it. In fact, I loved it. And I love you, Trevor, I really do. A part of me always will."

She stopped for a minute after saying that, realizing for the first time since she had approached Trevor in the bar he was finally beginning to look sober enough to understand her words.

"I wouldn't have done what I did with you unless I cared about you," Rose continued, fighting off a tear or two. "But here's the bottom line. You're not mine. You belong to someone else. I'm not sure how we happened, but I'm not sorry for it. It changed me for the better." She couldn't be certain, but she swore there was a tear in Trevor's eye as well. And not wanting to create a scene where they became two crying people in a bar, Rose stood tall, and finished what she came to do.

"You made a promise to someone, and I have a job to do. So you either walk out there and explain to that woman in a wedding gown who is waiting to become your bride why you won't be marrying her, or I will. I'm here on a mission and I better go back to work with some pictures of you saying *I Do* to Stephanie. You got yourself into this mess, and I'm trying to help you get out. It all happened for some kind of reason, I guess, but go out there and do what you need to do. And just so you know, this hasn't been easy for me either. But go, Trevor. Sober up, and go."

Rose almost felt as though she had given some kind of Oscar winning performance. Yes, this would be the clip from her life they played when they handed her the award one day. A triumph, a love lost, a conquering of herself and her career, all in one fail swoop. Yes, Rose was on top of her game today. And yet, she still had to get this man, whom she had once given her complete self to, to the altar in a very short time. To marry another woman. And she would photograph it all for a paycheck. And though she was just a little sad deep within, she couldn't help but laugh at the humor in it all.

Rose chastised Trevor into drinking the last of his coffee after her soliloquy, and he obeyed. She had no other choice than to treat him that way after what he had done, but she prided herself in knowing it all might have been a complete disaster had she not been there. Yes, she had almost died inside at the idea of losing him just a few hours before. But she surprised Frank and even herself at how she had reacted. She owned the situation, and saved the day in the process.

Rose only used her eyes to close their tab with the server. The rest of her body was entirely committed to seeing Trevor out of the bar and into his ceremony, wherever it would take place depending on the weather. She paid for the coffee they had together, as well as the for the beer Trevor had been drinking before she arrived. After all, he had paid for the beer she drank the night before Lily's funeral, and he had made sure she got back to her hotel room safely. Now, in return, she could pay for his cup of kindness and make sure he got back to his dressing room safely.

"So, am I ready to go now?"

"Well, almost. Let me wait for my receipt and then we'll go. You're not going anywhere without me."

"Yeah, I was kinda hoping for that."

"Do you want me to call Frank back? Because I can if I need to. He's only down the hall waiting on me to say the word."

"Simmer down, babe. I'm good. Really. Can we talk for just a second? Seriously." It honestly seemed as though he was striving for sincerity. And maybe even a bit of sobriety.

"You have about five minutes, Trevor. I swear, things are already off schedule here."

"If you love me, and I love you, then why are you pushing me to get married to someone else?"

"Trevor, I do love you. And I know that you love me. But we have different things that we want out of life. We're very different actually, we just have a truly unique attraction. I wouldn't change it, but we're just too different."

"I don't understand. I thought we had something. I mean, something good. Didn't we?"

"We do have something, Trevor. Maybe we always will. But it can't happen for us. You understand that, don't you?"

"I guess I understand. I just don't like it. I don't know what this means for me now."

They took hold of one another's hands.

"It means I'm taking a walk down the hall with you. It means you're getting married today, like was already planned. It means we're both leaving here a little confused, a little heartbroken, and even still a little in love. And it also means I'll never forget you. You'll never be far from me, no matter where you go, and deep down, I know I'll never be very far from you either."

Rose knew they had stalled a handful of times already, and they were stalling now. She looked at her watch anxiously, knowing the time was ticking by. Much too fast for her taste, and it left her little choice of what to do.

"Trevor, we have to leave now. It's time."

She stood up and reached for Trevor to steady him, just in case he wasn't stable on his own yet.

But Trevor stood up without incident, and Rose smiled at him. There were so many more words to say, and no time to say them. She hooked her arm inside his and began to walk down the hall toward their destiny. If anyone else saw them together, it would merely look as though Trevor were being a distinguished gentleman, escorting his high school friend and wedding photographer to the ceremony.

Rose walked Trevor to the door where the groomsmen were waiting until time for the wedding. She slowly took her arm away from Trevor's. She had never felt more proud of herself, and yet more strange inside. Maybe it really could have been them that day, she thought. Maybe, but it wasn't. They looked at one another and smiled as they separated. And that was the last time she spent with Trevor before he became a married man.

# CHAPTER NINETEEN

Still watching Trevor as he entered the room and reunited with the rest of his wedding party, Rose became misty-eyed. She slowly began to close the door and fade from view. But just before the door completely closed, Frank caught a glimpse of her. He jumped up to meet her, but she assured him things were fine. He looked into her eyes and still saw a bit of disturbance, but knew if she really needed him right now she would have said so. He trusted she would be true to herself at that moment. She delivered Trevor, and with that drama behind her, she returned to her assigned duties.

As she entered the bride's dressing room again, there was a low murmur. Word had apparently traveled quickly that Trevor was unable to be located earlier, and the ladies had begun to worry.

"Rose, is everything okay?" Stephanie asked in an concerned manner. "I heard no one could find Trevor. Where is he? Did someone find him?"

"He's fine, dear," Rose assured her with a smile.

"Where was he? Why was he gone?"

In an effort to settle the bride, Rose decided to say something that would not only ease Stephanie's mind, but also probably save the day as well. She certainly couldn't divulge what she had truly seen Trevor do and say. Thankfully, only she and Frank had seen that and no one else needed to know. Rose placed her hand on Stephanie's arm, in a comforting way, and explained how Trevor was still quite emotional over the recent loss of his father and sought some time alone to mourn his absence on such an important day. After all, his father was supposed to be his best man, and Rose knew more than she could say about how his death had affected Trevor. As she spoke, Rose listened to her own words leave her mouth, and watched her own hand rest on Stephanie's arm. The same hand which had just held on to Trevor's arm down the hall only moments ago.

"It's okay, Stephanie. It's all fine. Lots of emotions today from everyone. It's perfectly normal."

"Oh, well, I thought maybe he backed out. I'd actually wondered. Something seemed to be bothering him lately, even before his dad died. I don't know. But I appreciate you trying to keep me calm. It means a lot."

Rose wasn't sure what to say in return. She hadn't expected that confession from Stephanie. In a way she felt guilty, but then again not. Knowing Trevor had exhibited strange behavior in front of his fiancée before the wedding meant he was thinking of Rose more than she had realized. But Rose took a deep breath and continued on with her confusing afternoon. She couldn't imagine things ever being more awkward in her life than at that very second, but she had no idea what else was in store for that evening.

Frank entered the bride's dressing room, careful to make certain he wasn't catching anyone off guard.

"Everyone decent?"

The ladies loved Frank. He was handsome and engaging, and he complimented each one of them as he entered the room. The ladies had initially only wanted Rose in the private areas for photographing, but once they got to know Frank, they had changed their minds. Suddenly, their attention shifted to Frank and doing each and every little favor he asked. Stand here. Hold this. Move in closer. Rose was actually quite relieved. She needed something to fall into place and, thank goodness, Frank was making it happen here.

Rose glanced at her watch and noticed how so much time had seemingly disappeared over the course of the afternoon. She walked over to Frank and whispered that it was time for them to move along to the ceremony. They had just received word the ceremony would indeed take place outside, but with a very cloudy sky overhead. Still, it was the bride's preference to stay outdoors if at all possible, and so it would happen just that way. Rose wondered if it were some kind of omen, a cloudy sky with rain still in the distance, but it wasn't her decision to make. If they were happy with a cloudy wedding, then she would adjust her camera for the lack of natural lighting. Rose felt she might explode from all the highs and lows of emotions over the past few hours, but she managed to keep her composure.

Rose began her own walk down the stairs surrounding the waterfall, just as Stephanie would in a few minutes. She pretended to be the bride for a moment, imagining all eyes on her. She had always fought such a feeling, but at that moment in time, it felt quite nice.

Damn this cloudy wedding. Even the hint of a rainy sky reminded her of Lily. Rose allowed her mind to go places it shouldn't go right then. She thought of how Lily would never be a bride, and how she would never have the chance to make her beautiful bridal portrait. Oh, how lovely Lily would have looked in a wedding gown. Rose would never be her maid of honor. So much would never happen now and, yet, so much was getting ready to happen. Rose stood there all alone and looked up at the cloudy sky.

*"Oh Lily. You know the situation, and I know I don't need to bother explaining it all to you, thank goodness. Please help me on this cloudy day to get through all this, Lily. My sweet Lily, please."*

Rose grabbed the railing as she struggled to get a grip on her balance and on her soul. She walked down the bride's path, draped in white ribbons and soon to be covered by pink rose petals. As she descended the stairs, she saw Frank standing near where the groom would be standing. It seemed weird to think of him there, that way. Like a groom. She paused for a moment as he looked up through the lens of his camera and snapped a few pictures. Pictures of her.

"Don't do that," she said quietly, hoping he would read the message from her lips. "I'm not the bride."

But Frank couldn't help himself. He thought she looked lovely. He snapped a few more pictures of her before she sent him a threatening look. Frank knew precisely what it meant, and he lowered his camera from his face.

"Okay, okay." Frank winked at her and grinned. Rose silently wondered if even she realized just how much these two men were making her crazy.

As Rose met Frank at the foot of the waterfall, he reached down and kissed her on the head. Whenever he did, it always reminded her that they were friends first, before anything else. She took great comfort in that. They watched together as the guests arrived and were seated. Before Rose knew it, the families were being seated. Then it was time for the processional. She and Frank picked up their cameras and, in their professional way, began to move about the beautifully decorated ceremony site. They were unobtrusive and almost went unnoticed.

As Trevor and his groomsmen stepped out from the side, Rose felt a strange combination of relief and angst. She glanced at him quickly, but only on her way to get a better view of the bridesmaids. She thought eye contact at this point might not only be unsettling, but perhaps even a bit dangerous. Rose was never one to cry at weddings. So when she felt herself fighting off the tears it was unclear whether they were from the beauty and magic of all which takes place at such an event, or from the idea that Trevor would no longer be within her reach. No longer an option. No longer a possibility of being hers.

Trevor and his groomsmen stood ready as the music played. The bridesmaids filed in one by one, and then the ring bearer and flower girl. And finally, she turned to see the bride ready to make her entrance. The stage was all set, the players just seemed wrong. At least to Rose. The music began for the bride's procession, and there was Stephanie, ready to take that walk.

Rose admitted she looked beautiful, but she had the strangest demeanor. As Stephanie walked down the steps beside the waterfall, she kept looking around at the scenery and the decorations, and never really fixated on her groom. Rose kept waiting for that moment when the bride and groom first looked at each other and locked eyes. But when it happened, finally, it just wasn't the dramatic instance Rose and her camera had waited for.

Still, Rose captured some excellent pictures of them exchanging their vows as she knelt with a view of Trevor's face. She watched as they spoke to each other, promising to love and honor one another all the days of their lives. Just as Stephanie turned to her maid of honor to get Trevor's wedding band, Rose saw him whisper the words "I love you." Rose thought it was meant for Stephanie, but why would he have waited until she had her head turned to say it? Then she saw him look directly at *her*.

Had he really just whispered he loved *her* in the middle of his wedding to Stephanie? Thankfully, everyone thought it was meant for his bride, including Stephanie who happened to hear him even though she didn't see him say it. Rose continued to view it all from behind her lens, and was thankful it kept anyone from seeing her own face. And so, there at the foot of the waterfall on that grey summer day, Trevor and Stephanie were married.

Everyone made their way inside the hotel to the reception area, and Rose watched as they cut the cake, had their first dance, and were toasted by several friends and family. And just like the night of Lily's wake, Rose looked on as Trevor made a beautiful and poignant toast. This time in memory of his father who had recently passed. There wasn't a dry eye in the house, except for Stephanie, who seemed oddly unaffected. She did reach over and slightly touch his hand for a moment, but it just didn't seem like enough to Rose. Out of sheer respect for seeing someone so sad, Rose wanted to hold his hand to keep it all from hurting him so much. But his hand was no longer hers to hold.

Rose was glad when the music started back up again and everyone moved towards the dance floor. The mood had grown quite heavy with all the emotional toasts. Stephanie pulled Trevor out on the floor, though he looked a tad resistant, and still teary from his toast. As the floor filled up with dancers of every age, Rose watched from behind her lens. She felt someone walk up next to her, and she took the camera away from her face. There stood Frank.

"Is your dance card full, or might I have the pleasure of finding myself on the dance floor with you?"

Rose loved that he knew what a dance card was. He was a wonderful blend of yesterday and today, old-fashioned and modern.

"I'd love to dance with you, and my dance card does seem to have some openings."

Rose stood up and gave her hand to Frank, and they joined the others on the floor.

As they danced, they laughed, smiled, and had a few light moments together, which were much needed after the day they had experienced. When Rose felt a tap on her shoulder, she thought it was Frank trying to trick her into turning around, so she didn't look. Then she felt a second tap, and Frank nodded his head for Rose to look behind her. There stood Trevor and Stephanie.

"May we cut in?" Trevor asked.

Frank took a few seconds to agree, waiting for Rose's approval before he took Stephanie as his dance partner. Stephanie giggled and blushed as Frank put his arm behind her back and began to dance with her. Rose and Trevor just watched them for a few moments.

"He's quite the ladies' man, isn't he?"

"Well, the ladies do seem to love him. He's a great guy. But then again, so are you, Trevor."

"Rose, I'm sorry about you finding me in the bar today. I had so much on my mind, and all I really wanted to do was talk to you."

"Trevor, we need to dance instead of just standing here talking on the floor."

"Yeah, I suppose we do."

Trevor slipped his arm behind Rose, touching her for the first time since he had become Stephanie's husband. Rose wanted it to feel different. She wanted it to feel wrong. But it didn't. It felt as wonderful as always. And though it was their first time to dance together, no one would have guessed by watching them.

"Anyhow, Rose, I'm sorry. I always had my dad to talk to about things like this, and it's been so tough since he died."

Trevor looked down and watched his shiny black dress shoes move next to Rose's smaller dainty black pumps.

"I know, Trevor. And just in case it comes up later, I told Stephanie the same thing. She somehow learned you were missing in action around the hotel earlier, and I told her you had just needed some alone time because you missed your father."

"You did that? For me? I didn't deserve such a favor, you know. And Rose, please don't judge me for what I'm about to say. I know

I'm married now, but I'll always love you. A gal in a white dress and a five layer cake doesn't change anything in my mind or in my heart. But I know we're getting ready to go our separate ways."

Rose honestly had no idea how to respond. She looked over her shoulder and saw Frank sweeping Stephanie off her feet, making her laugh and smile, and then turned back to look at Trevor. At least she had this moment to speak with him while Frank was occupying the bride. This might be the last chance she ever had to talk with Trevor alone, and though she had so much to say, she could barely speak.

"I told you, Trevor, we'll always be special to each other. And we'll always be a part of each other."

Trevor took his arm from behind her, stepped back, and twirled Rose back into his arms. They even had chemistry on the dance floor, not just in the bedroom. Suddenly, all eyes turned to them. People assumed Trevor was showing off, like he was known to do, by spinning the magazine photographer around. Everyone had a good time around Trevor, and that's all this appeared to be – a good time. They talked, and laughed, and danced, and spoke one last time. When the dance ended, Frank delivered Stephanie back to her groom, and Trevor stepped away from Rose, bowing in an old-fashioned way to his dance partner. It was nothing like the Trevor she knew. Maybe he was different around her. Maybe Rose did make him different when they were together. Still, there stood his bride, and there stood Frank. Trevor reached down to give Rose a peck on the cheek.

"Thanks to you both for all your work tonight," Trevor said, and he reached over to shake Frank's hand. "Can't wait to see the magazine photos."

"Our pleasure," Frank said as he shook Trevor's hand. They didn't speak any other words. Then, Frank bowed to Stephanie, just as Trevor had done to Rose, and thanked her for the dance.

"Yes, thanks for the *dance*, Rose," Trevor said. Rose understood he had said the word dance as a reference to all they had shared together, and she just nodded her head and smiled. And when she thought about it, their time together had been like a dance, moving back and forth and all around. She also thought he looked *so* nice in his tuxedo. And at the same time, Trevor had thought how sexy it had been to see Rose in action all evening, as she took pictures and mingled through the crowd. They looked at each other once more, and wondered when, or even if, they might ever see each other again. As they said goodbye, Stephanie took Trevor's arm and moved to another part of the dance floor. Frank looked at Rose's sweet, confused face.

"Rose, can I talk to you outside for a minute? Please?"

## CHAPTER TWENTY

Rose was so nervous she had done something on the dance floor with Trevor that had upset Frank.

"Is everything okay, Frank?"

"I just want to step outside for a few minutes. Please, join me."

Rose thought it sounded strange. But he extended his arm toward the balcony door, and she began to walk in that direction.

Frank had waited all evening for the perfect moment. This looked as good as any other.

They arrived at the French doors which led out to the reception room balcony. Frank opened the door and then closed it behind them when they were both outside. The balcony overlooked not only the waterfall, but also the lake. They both took a moment to breathe in the evening air. Tired and warm from their work, and from being surrounded by a room packed full of guests, the fresh air felt like heaven.

"Rose…"

"Yes, Frank?"

"You were amazing today, Rose. That's just one of the things I wanted to tell you. But really, you were just amazing today. You overcame so much to still do a professional job tonight. I know I can't fully understand everything you felt today, but I know it was excruciating for you at times. And yet you still captured wonderful pictures, I'm sure. You held your head high, and kept your wits about you. It's a small wonder you didn't fall apart. I honestly think I might have."

"I don't know what to say, Frank. You taught me how to be the consummate professional."

"Well, maybe you learned that from me, but I've never been through a day like the one you had today. I don't know if I could have handled things as well as you did. You were amazing today Rose, and I wanted to express my admiration."

"Thank you, Frank. But what can I say? I learned from the master."

"Rose, I have something for you."

Frank nervously reached into his pocket and got down on one knee in front of Rose.

Rose felt stunned, and in shock. Was Frank getting ready to propose to her? She didn't think she was ready for a commitment, and definitely wasn't prepared to tell him yes, or even no.

"Rose, my family is of Irish descent. This is a Claddagh ring," he said, as he pulled the ring box out of his pocket and opened it before her. "It has a crown, hands, and a heart which stand for friendship, loyalty and love.

"It doesn't mean we're engaged or anything. I mean, it *could*, but the ring is meant to be worn according to how it is given. It can be worn in friendship, a relationship, an engagement, or marriage. It was given by my grandmother to my mother, and as an only child, my mother passed it to me to give to a special woman one day. Rose, I want you to have it. You've been the best friend I've ever had, and certainly the best woman I've ever known. I mean, outside of my mother." And he stopped as they both laughed a little.

"Whether or not we stay together, I want you to have it. If you'll wear it, it would be on the right hand. If you want to merely accept it in friendship, then wear the ring with the crown pointing towards your heart. If you want to consider a relationship with me, then wear it with the crown pointing away from the heart. It's up to you, and I'll respect and admire you, no matter which way you choose to wear it."

Rose carefully extended her right hand to Frank, and he was so pleased she would accept the ring in *any* way he offered it. As he began to slip it onto her right ring finger with the crown pointing towards her heart, assuming that's the direction she would choose, Rose shook her head back and forth. She used her left hand to reposition the ring in the other direction, and Frank slid the ring on her finger.

"Are you sure, Rose? I didn't mean any pressure here. Honest."

"I'm quite certain, my dear. I mean, I'm not sure where all this is going either, you understand. But I'm ready to find out."

Rose held it in the moonlight and tilted it back and forth, watching the appropriately colored rose stone inside the silver setting sparkle. "It's beautiful. Just beautiful."

Frank lifted Rose up and twirled her around in the moonlight with both her feet dangling in the air. After a tumultuous and tiresome day, this was a light and celebratory moment for them both. He kissed her passionately and then slowly lowered her to the ground. It was a perfect ending to what Rose earlier thought would be a perfect mess of a day.

Rose had no idea Trevor was inside the reception still, watching everything they did from a distance through the balcony window. Not understanding the meaning of the ring or the circumstances under which it was given by Frank or received by Rose, and not even noticing which hand the ring had been placed on, Trevor assumed the two were now engaged. He felt mad, and sad, and devastated. The idea that Frank would make love to her that night made him feel sick. He might be married to Stephanie, but at least in his mind, he would still be making love to Rose.

In complete frustration, Trevor walked across the room, took his bride's hand, and whispered in her ear.

"I want to go upstairs to our room, Stephanie. *Now*."

She was unknowingly impressed by his demand, and giggled to some of the guests.

"Duty calls," she then said, and excused herself from their chat.

Stephanie headed toward the door with Trevor, thinking he was merely anxious for their honeymoon to begin. Just as he walked through the doorway, he braced his hand against the wall and stopped. He backed up, and reached for the bar. He grabbed a bottle of champagne, two glasses, and left his own wedding reception a broken-hearted man.

Frank and Rose, however, returned to their room to celebrate. Not only the end of a successful six week stint away from the office, but also of the exploration of their relationship. They would return home with a fabulously executed assignment, knowing more of what they meant to one another, and ready to face life better than they left it a few weeks ago.

The next morning, as Rose began to check out, she was given a note by the hotel desk clerk. It was from Trevor. It merely read *Congratulations*.

Rose stared at it blankly, wondering what he meant. Then she realized Trevor must have seen her out on the balcony the night before and assumed Frank had proposed marriage.

"What is it, Rose?"

She showed him the note. Frank read it and knew it was upsetting to Rose, so he kissed her on the head and held her close.

Rose looked at the clerk with the note from Trevor still clutched in her hand.

"Have the bride and groom from last night checked out yet?"

"Yes ma'am, they did. Quite early this morning, in fact."

Rose wasn't sure why she asked. Maybe she could try to explain it all to Trevor. But, in a way, she was actually relieved to know they had already left.

"We can't wait to see the pictures in the magazine, Ms. Millican. It was a pleasure having you all at our hotel."

"Thank you for everything. It was lovely being here again."

Rose and Frank loaded their equipment and luggage in their car and headed towards home. The rain which had been looming over them since late last night finally began to fall. Rose rested in the passenger seat while Frank drove, and sat tilting the ring back and forth and watching it sparkle. Frank glanced at her while she admired the ring over and over. He desperately needed her friendship and companionship. He never wanted to lose her in any capacity. He knew for now she carried him in her heart as a friend, and a lover, and possibly one day, even more. But he still longed for a more permanent answer.

"Frank…"

"Yes, love?"

"I'd like to stop by Lily's grave before we leave town. I haven't been since the funeral, and I honestly don't know when I'll be back again. I'd like to stop while I'm still here."

"I think that sounds like a wonderful idea, Rose. I'd be happy to take you there. But it's raining, you know."

"I know," Rose replied with a smile. "Seems like it almost always is." ---

# ABOUT THE AUTHOR

Michele Pendleton was born in Chattanooga, Tennessee and studied Communications: Journalism at the University of Tennessee at Chattanooga where she received her Bachelor of Arts degree. Michele has written numerous novels, poems, and short stories, and "Rose, On Her Own" is her first published novel. She lives in Huntsville, Alabama with her husband, Joel.

Made in the USA
Lexington, KY
04 June 2013